WAHIDA CLARK PRESENTS

SWAG II

BY

WAHIDA CLARK
WITH
ANGEL SANTOS

Wahida Clark Presents Publishing
60 Evergreen Place
Suite 904A
East Orange, New Jersey 07018
1-866-910-6920

www.wclarkdistribution.com
www.wclarkpublishing.com

Library of Congress Cataloging-In-Publication Data:

Wahida Clark
Swag II
ISBN 13-digit: 9781947732452
ISBN 10-digit: 9781947732469

1. Sex-Trafficking- 2. Transgender- 3. New Orleans- 4. Hurricane Katrina- 5. Lesbians- 6. LBGT- 7. Drug Trafficking

Creative direction & layout by Art Supplied Gfx
Acreativenuance.com

Printed in USA

WAHIDA CLARK PRESENTS

SWAG II

-1-

It was like taking candy from a baby.

"Girl, that nigguh got it! I'm tellin' you, get on it because he trickin' like a muhfucka!" Tammy, the waitress, exclaimed.

"Who?" Tosha asked with the intensity of a fiend searching for her next fix.

"I ain't gonna point . . . but him . . . The high-yellow nigguh in the glasses and bow tie . . . Poindexter!" Tammy giggled at her own joke.

When Tosha locked in on him, her eyeballs rolled like a slot machine, stopping on dollar signs, like: Jackpot!

He was definitely a Poindexter. From a distance, she couldn't tell how he looked, but the corny cut of his expensive clothes told her two things: he had money and he was totally green, her favorite combination.

"I'm on it. Good lookin', Tam." Tosha winked.

"Uh-uh, ain't no good lookin'. You know the drill. Break me off," Tammy demanded with her hand out.

Her hustle was to direct strippers to ballers before the other strippers moved in on them. She fucked with everyone, but Tosha paid the best. Tosha dropped a fifty in her fly trap palm.

"I wasn't gonna forget."

"I wasn't gonna let you."

Tosha slid off the stool and strutted across the room. With her partner and number one competition, Mona, having been murdered, she was by far the thickest, sexiest red-bone stallion in the club.

More for me, had been her reaction when she heard Mona got killed. Tosha had the heart of a cold-blooded bitch, the body of a bad bitch, and the face of an angel. Lord have mercy on any man in her sights.

And Poindexter was definitely in her sights.

She put her stiletto with the strap that crisscrossed her calf, on his seat, right between his legs so her toes brushed his balls, and said, "You want a dance, baby?"

"My God!" he gasped when he laid eyes on her.

He downed his drink, took off his glasses, and wiped them on his shirt, then put them back on.

"You are *beautiful!*"

She smiled seductively before sitting down on his lap, facing him.

"I'll take that as a yes."

"H-how much?" he stammered, holding a fan of one-hundred-dollar bills.

"Two of these," she replied, plucking two bills and making double what she usually made.

Her fat, juicy titties sat close to his lips, all he had to do was pucker up and he'd kiss them. He looked at them, damn near salivating.

"Are these . . . real?"

She had to stifle a giggle. His lameness was too good to be true.

"Real expensive," she retorted and began to grind his dick.

Damn, Poindexter's holding, she thought as his dick came to life. She was like a snake charmer; she could make any cobra spit.

Looking at his face, Tosha could see he wasn't half bad. In fact, he looked damn good. He was an albino white, like a sheet. His red hair was cut short and waved to the side, old school style. Brown freckles dotted his face giving him a youthful look. But his eyes . . .

If the eyes were windows to the soul, then his had to be pitch black . . . or non-existent. They peered at her lustfully . . . intently . . . amused . . . They say love is blind, but greed is worse. It makes you see what isn't there and ignore what is.

"You like that, daddy?"

His eyes seemed to roll up in the back of his head, as his body jerked once . . . twice and then went still.

"Did you just—"

"I'm–I'm sorry. I couldn't help it. Here, take one more," he offered, handing her another big face.

She gobbled it up in one chuck. "Listen," she began, running her nail along his cheek, "if you're trying to spend some real money, we can go in the VIP room and–"

"Oh no, I'd be too embarrassed with other people around."

"Believe me, daddy, you ain't got nothin' to be embarrassed about."

"I–I–I have a room near here."

Tosha shook her head. "No, baby, we can do the same thing in VIP."

He looked at her eagerly. "I–I won't be able to perform, but I'm willing to pay you two thousand to . . . to have sex with me," he offered, then dropped his head as if he were ashamed he said it.

Her greedy mind cackled like the wicked witch, but her composure remained unruffled.

"I usually get three thousand," she lied smoothly.

He nodded vigorously, then dug in his pocket, producing a wad of money.

"You're worth it all." He smiled.

Her pussy got slick just from the sight of the hundred-dollar bills. She kissed him softly on the lips.

"I'ma treat you *real* good, daddy. Let me get my things," she told him, standing up. "I'll be right back. Don't go anywhere."

"I won't."

He waited . . .

As soon as they entered his room, Tosha was all over him. Now that the three-grand was in her purse, she was working on making him cum like an ATM on the fritz.

"Hey, slow down," he snickered. "Would you like a drink?"

She grabbed a handful of dick. "Of this," Tosha cooed.

"Then . . . take off your clothes," he told her.

"Whatever you say, daddy," she replied, stepping back so he could see her peel out of her tiny tank top and miniskirt. She stood totally naked, except for her heels.

"The shoes, too."

"I like 'em on," she teased.

"I don't," he replied, his voice firmer than it had been.

The sound of his rich baritone chilled and thrilled her.

"Okay," she complied.

She took off her shoes, even though she didn't want to. Without her heels, she felt vulnerable.

"Now, get on your hands and knees and crawl to me, you dog ass bitch!" he commanded, his voice rumbling.

The remark threw her off. *Poindexter?*

"What did you——"

Smack!

He backhanded her so hard, gravity was the only thing that kept her from taking flight, but it didn't stop her from spinning like a top and hitting the carpet, face first.

"Nigguh, I'll kill you!" she shouted.

Tosha wasn't a stallion for nothing. She was hood born and bred, so if he thought she was going out like the last bitch, he had his people fucked up.

Tosha jumped and grabbed her purse, snatching the straight razor out. He could've stopped her if he wanted, but he watched her with cold amusement. When she finally flicked it out, he chuckled.

"Bitch, I'm gonna make you eat that razor," he said, then took off his glasses.

Glasses are amazingly deceptive. Clark Kent, a timid librarian, changed into Superman, just as Poindexter, the nerdy nympho changed into the devil himself. She looked into the cold marble that was his eyes and *wished* she hadn't pulled the razor. Now that it was out, she knew there was no turning back.

"Aahh!" she hollered, lunging at him and slicing the air, but not him.

He side stepped the downward arc of her arm, then hit her where a woman is weakest. The stomach. He hit her as hard as he'd hit a man, knocking all the wind and fight out of her. She dropped the razor and her ass to the floor, gasping for air.

He casually bent to pick up the razor then squatted down and lifted her face by her hair. The well-placed smack had only reddened and swollen her cheek. A temporary disfigurement, but he held the razor to her face and threatened a permanent one.

"Bitch, let me introduce myself. I am now the proud owner of your sorry, dog ass. Greedy bitch! That three-grand bought you." He chuckled. "Now, my name is Satan, but since you're a pretty bitch, you can call me daddy."

"Ple–please," Tosha whined, looking into the cold black onyx of his glare.

He ignored her plea, stood up, walked across the room, then turned back to her.

"Now grab your purse and crawl your worthless ass across the burning hot sands and maybe, just maybe, I'll make a true bitch out of you," he hissed so coldly her skin got goose bumps.

Tosha clutched the purse and slowly, shakily, and painfully, crawled to him.

"Now kiss my gators," Satan demanded.

She puckered and put her lips upon his reptile.

He smiled. "Now . . . where's your offering?"

She handed up the purse.

Satan pulled the money out and thumbed through it.

"Shit, most of this is mine anyway, but I'ma take it . . . for now," he replied, then turned for the door. "Now it's time I break you in."

When he opened the door, three thugs walked in, leering.

"Just don't bruise the bitch. I already got a sale for her. Brand her and put her on ice. I'm goin' back out. The waitress looked tasty." He chuckled, then added, "Like taking candy from a baby."

Satan walked out. When Tosha looked up, all she saw were gold teeth and big dicks. They looked like they were holding bats to beat her with. One of the thugs got behind her and tried to rearrange her guts with one thrust.

"Goddamn, this pussy wet!" he grunted, spreading her ample ass cheeks so he could watch his snake slither in and out of her center.

"Oooohhhh!" she tried to moan, more out of pain than pleasure, but the "O" of her lips was filled till the corners of her mouth hurt and her throat gagged on pure mule dick.

"Aaarrgghh!" the two thugs see-sawed the bitch in and out, dicks so deep in her, they damn near met in her chest, and when they came, their sperm had to have charged at each other like two angry armies.

The three of them fucked her until her every orifice was red, swollen, and sore. She prayed if she could only make it out alive, she'd change her life . . . but sometimes, second chances aren't likely. When they finished, one of the thugs pulled out something that looked like a potato masher, but with a switch like a curler. After a few minutes, the wire design glowed red with heat. Tosha never saw it coming. She lay on the floor on her stomach, cum on her chin, and oozing from her ass and pussy. Suddenly, two of the thugs each grabbed an arm. The thug with the branding iron sat on her legs. They knew once that heat hit her, she'd buck to get away. But she didn't. She was too tired and too broken.

Sssssssssssss!

The iron hissed when he put it to her left ass cheek. Her whole body tensed, but she had nothing left to cry out with. The smell of burning flesh reminded them of pork chops and Cajun summer nights. When he removed the iron, he pulled out an airplane bottle of gin, took a short swig then doused the brand with alcohol. This time she did moan, low and deep, like the beginning of an old Negro spiritual.

He looked at his handiwork, the alcohol bubbling away any chance of infection.

"Perfect. Let's get her to the car."

The brand stood out red and sizzling on her pecan tone. Now she officially belonged to Satan.

It was the symbol of the double dragon.

-2-

"You're like . . . a thug superhero or something," Rain remarked, as she sat on the queen-sized bed watching Jazmine stand in the mirror and transform into Swag. It had been a year since she was promoted to detective. While she preferred narcotics, this position landed her in the homicide department, which worked for her as well.

Jasmine laughed after putting in the green contacts.

"I'm serious, Jaz," Rain continued, then deepened her voice. "Cop by day, gangsta by night. Da–da–daa Swag!"

Her expression was playful, but Jazmine knew there was something more to it, when she added, "For real, yo. Do you ever know who you are?"

Inside, Rain was feeling like, *Do I even know who I am?*

Jazmine paused before putting on the moustache and goatee. She sat down next to Rain on the bed and took her hand.

"Ma . . . I know this is hard for you, but—"

"How can you, Jaz? Huh? You *knew* who you were when you made me fall in love with you, but *I* didn't! I thought you were a fuckin' man! *My* man! Then I thought you were a faggot, and I find out you're a woman! A *woman*, Jaz, I'm in love with a woman! I'm not gay!" Rain cried, tears streaming down her cheeks.

To say she was confused was an understatement. Imagine meeting the person of your dreams, falling in love, and then finding out this person is the same sex as you!

Jasmine tried to wipe the tears away, but Rain shoved her hand away. Jazmine sighed.

"I . . . I didn't plan on falling in love with you either, Rain, but we can't choose who we love. I mean . . . what is gay anyway? Why so many labels? We're *human* and we fuckin' fell in love and for once don't regret it."

"Fuck you, Jaz. I want some dick!"

Jazmine smirked.

"Well, I haven't put it on yet, but if you check the dresser . . ."

Rain glared at her but couldn't keep a straight face. She burst out laughing.

"I hate when you do that!" she exclaimed, laughing and crying at the same time. She fell back on the bed, covering her face with her hands. "I'm sooooo fuckin' confused!"

Jazmine lay on top of her and kissed her passionately.

"Just love me, Rain. We'll figure this thing out together."

Rain gazed into her green eyes, the green eyes she fell in love with, until she remembered they were fake.

"Jaz! Jaz! I wanna wear your moustache!" Malaya yelled out, hop-scotching into the room.

Jazmine scooped her up, making her squeal with delight. She sat her on the bed, then handed her the moustache/goatee disguise. Malaya held it to her face. She looked like a bearded midget. Rain laughed.

"Say the line, Né-Né!" she urged her. Amused that her daughter got a kick out of watching the old seventies sitcom Different Strokes.

"What you talkin' about, Willis!" Malaya said in the deepest voice her little self could muster.

Rain and Jazmine fell out laughing. When their eyes met, they knew they were having a family moment, and neither could deny how good it felt.

"Remember, Mé-Mé, you can never, ever, ever, tell anybody Jaz has a moustache, right?" Jazmine reminded her.

"I remember," Malaya sang, handing it back to Jaz.

"And who's the dude that lives here?"

"Swag!"

"That's right. That's our secret," Jazmine said, tickling Malaya's stomach. Then she looked at Rain and added, "Our *family* secret."

Rain just looked at her, then playfully slapped Malaya's bottom.

"Okay, little girl, go get ready for your bath."

"Okay, Mommy!"

She skipped out. Jazmine went to the dresser.

"Jaz," Rain called her.

"What?"

"Leave the dick."

Jazmine smirked.

"What if I—"

"Leave it," Rain cut her off, hating herself for being so weak.

Jazmine applied the moustache and goatee, checked it in the mirror, then turned to kiss Rain. Rain turned her head.

"Don't kiss me with that thing on."

Jazmine nodded understandingly.

"I love you."

"Yeah," Rain replied, folding her arms, but when Jazmine walked out, she mumbled, "I love you too."

Jazmine backed the motorcycle out of the kitchen and down the plank of wood she had over the back steps. She kept it in the house because she didn't want anybody who knew her as Swag, stumbling across his bike. She threw on her helmet, gunned the bike, then pulled around to the front of her condo. When she reached the parking lot, she looked around then sped off.

"Shit!" Matson exclaimed.

As soon as the bike zoomed by, he knew it was her. He just didn't know that the 'her' was now a 'him.' But he could tell from the bikers build that it was Jazmine. Only problem was, there was no way he could pursue her without being detected. He didn't have that problem with her car. However, he knew she had got hip to the tail he would put on her sometime, so he decided to put a small GPS chip under the rear bumper. Matson was on her because he wanted her. Wanted her bad. There was no doubt in his mind that she had something to do with Detective Hall's death. He knew she had something to do with the bodies found in the cemetery. He also knew she was dirty, but he couldn't prove it. As they say, it's not what you know, it's what you can prove, and Matson was determined to prove it.

Having lost Jazmine for the time being, he decided to get out, take a look around, and figure out how he had overlooked the motorcycle. He stepped lightly, careful of the Neighborhood Watch, thinking how ironic it would be if someone called the police. He followed the bike tracks to the back of the house. When he saw the makeshift ramp over the stairs, he knew why he'd missed the bike. She kept it in the house.

"Smart," he remarked with grudging approval.

He glanced through the kitchen window, thinking of the plain view doctrine. Nothing. He walked around the other side of the condo, so hungry for something, *anything*, he'd become a peeping Tom.

And then he got an eyeful.

"Ooohhhh fuck!" Rain sang, sliding the thick, black ten-inch dildo inside of her wet pussy.

Matson froze.

As a cop, he knew he should look away, but as a man, he just couldn't. She was totally naked, chocolate, dark chocolate, darker chocolate than his chocolate wife and much, *much* thicker. Lying on her back, her ass was so fat she had to arch her back to keep her shoulders on the bed. Her legs were spread wide, knees up, and heels digging into the bed for leverage. In a word, she was sex. Her lips parted with the sweetest moan he had ever heard.

He was stuck, his dick hardened to full length instantly, and for a second, a split second, he had a tremendous urge to smash through the window, snatch the dildo out her hand and replace it with his own dick.

"Oh, fuck me harder. Put it all in," she cooed, pushing the entire dildo inside of her until her knuckle brushed her clit.

She cocked her leg back, her sexy ass foot arched as if wearing a Louboutin as she fucked herself vigorously.

Matson found himself with his dick in his hand, pumping just as furiously. He had never been so turned on in his life. Maybe it was the allure of the forbidden, the thrill of the voyeur, that made breaking the law so sexy. But for that moment he gripped and pumped his rock-hard bone, imagining Rain calling out his name instead of, "Swag. Oh, fuck me, Swag. I love youuuuu!"

Her pussy swallowed each ten-inch thrust, wanting more, deeper, longer. She teetered, tantalizing on the edge of fisting herself. Her pussy was on fire.

"Harder, baby, I'm almost, a-al-almost . . ." She gasped. Then just as her body stiffened, bucked and shook, she cried out, "Oh, Jazmine!"

Jazmine?

Matson's load hit the wall with a splat! Clinging to the aluminum siding, frantically swimming around like, "Where the fuck are we? This ain't the uterus!"

His knees felt like jelly. Back in his right mind, now flooded by shame and embarrassment, he slunk off and headed for his car.

Jazmine?

Why did she call out Jazmine when she came? he wondered. The Swag name sounded like a dude, her boyfriend maybe, but Jazmine . . .

As he drove, the thought stayed in his mind. Maybe Jazmine was a dyke . . . No . . . the way she played the game, she wasn't a dyke. Bi maybe, but definitely not a dyke.

##########

When Matson walked through the door, he was greeted by a chorus of, "Daddy!" as his two girls rushed to hug him. He dropped to one knee and hugged them both, happy to be a daddy, a husband, and a black man in love.

"We missed you, Daddy!" his five-year-old, Felecity, said, kissing his cheek.

"We love you, Daddy!" his twelve-year-old, Bianca, chimed in.

He smiled knowingly.

"Okay, what's with the Hallmark commercial? No, you're not getting a pony," he told Felecity. "No, you're not getting your ears pierced yet," he told Bianca, then looked at his wife coming out of the kitchen, and said, "No, we're not going to Jamaica."

His wife Sonia laughed then gave him a kiss.

"Hello to you too, Tony." "No, Daddy, I don't want my ears—well I do, but I really want to go see the OMG Girlz. Please, Daddy! That will be my birthday weekend!" Bianca begged.

"OMG Girlz?" he echoed, looking at Sonia.

"They're this little girl group. The girls love them." She told him

"Please, Daddy!"

"I want to go, too," Felecity huffed.

"You can go . . ." he began, and the girls broke into wild cheers. He held up a finger and they stopped, barely able to control their excitement. "*If* you're in bed and asleep in ten minutes."

They disappeared up the stairs so quickly, he thought he saw cartoon wind streaks behind them.

"OMG Girlz need to come to town more often." He laughed, pulling Sonia into his arms.

He kissed her with a kiss that made her pussy tingle. When they broke it, she looked at him, smiling mischievously.

"Somebody's been thinkin' about me."

Somebody . . .

Matson gripped her ass.

"All day long."

"You know, I've got this new teddy."

"No."

"No?"

"No teddy. Just you, butt naked and sweaty," he replied, sucking her neck.

Sonia bit her bottom lip.

"Sounds serious."

"It's crucial."

She felt his rock-hard dick against her stomach.

"Come show me," she teased, taking him by the hand and leading him upstairs.

His eyes followed the sway of her ass as he walked up the stairs behind her, ready to fuck the shit out of Rain . . .

I mean . . . his wife.

-3-

Swag entered the Pink Diamond, attracting love like a magnet in a room full of metal. Boys wanted kisses and girls wanted hugs, never knowing that Swag was bringing the straightness out of gay dudes and crookedness out of straight females. Her sexuality was so fluid, it made her laugh to herself, seeing how little people truly knew themselves.

"Hello, you fine motherfucker," Derrick, the fruity owner of the club, greeted Swag.

Swag kissed him playfully, slipping tongue in Derrick's mouth, making him coo like a pigeon.

"Boy, don't play with me. Have me bent over this bar," Derrick flirted, looking as light as a ballet dancer.

"You should make that the name of a drink. Where's Miss Toni?"

Derrick's eyes got serious. "In the basement."

Swag understood the hidden meaning.

"Everything good up here?"

"Always," Derrick replied.

Swag dipped through the special exit door beside the bar. It led to a staircase that descended deep below the club, sewer level. The farther she went, the darker it got, and the music became more muted, until the thump of the bass sounded like a distant heartbeat. She came to an old black door and knocked. Several seconds later, one of the twins, Milly, answered the door.

"'Allo love. Toni's been expectin' ya."

Swag stepped into the cold and dimly lit room. The scent of sewage and the shriek of hungry rats filled the air. In the middle of the room, under the single hanging light bulb was a chair. In the chair was a man. Bloody. Swollen. Hands and feet tied to the chair. The other twin, Lilly, stood holding the leash of a pit in one hand and a metal pipe in the other. The pit bull breathed hard, blood dripping from his powerful jaw. The man's legs were mangled and bitten down to the bone. Miss Toni, in heels impossibly arched, strutted before him back and forth.

"And now you're beginning to piss me off. So, I'm gonna ask one more—Oh, hey baby. I was just getting warmed up," he said when he saw Swag.

He kissed her on the cheek.

Swag eyed the bloodied victim. "This would go a whole lot easier if you'd just cooperate," Swag remarked.

"And just like I told this mangy looking faggot, I'm tellin' you! You might as well kill me 'cause I ain't sayin' shit!" he growled, the pain and anger playing tag in his veins.

"He ain't break, I'll give him that," Miss Toni remarked.

Swag looked at him for a moment before squatting down eye level and studying his swollen face. He glared back at her through blackened eyes.

"Tough guy, huh? You a real nigguh, ready to rep till the end. I respect that." Swag nodded. "Ain't too many of y'all left. You a dying breed."

He didn't say anything, but she could tell her words were gassing his ego.

"So I'ma tell you what I'm gonna do . . . I'ma let you go," Swag said.

He looked at her, a spark of hope in his eyes, but it quickly disappeared once she added, "After I fuck you."

Lilly cackled and Miss Toni howled, but Swag didn't crack a smile.

"I'm not gonna just fuck you in this basement; I'm gonna fuck you all over the world, on World Star,

Facebook, and Instagram. Everybody you know and everybody who knows you is gonna see you bent over taking every inch of this dick."

"Nig—nigguh fuck you!" he fumed, because it was the only thing he could think of, and his ego said he had to say something. He was a thug's thug, a gangsta. Pain was nothing . . . but his pride was everything . . . he would die to keep his pride and Swag knew that.

Swag chuckled.

"Yeah . . . think about it. Everybody gonna see it. Sure, you're tied up, but what you think will look worse: muhfuckas knowin' you got raped like a bitch or got fucked like a faggot?" Swag kept his gaze on the die-hard soldier. "Lilly, wiped his face. I want everybody to see when he starts to realize he likes it. Then we'll let him go."

He wanted to hold his water, but he couldn't live with knowing that everybody would see him getting fucked. His pride couldn't take it.

Lilly wiped his face. Miss Toni motioned for Milly. Milly pushed the chair over, causing the gangsta thug to thump onto the concrete. He groaned in pain. The pit bulls barked hoping they would get to feast. She kicked the chair away, and her and Lilly dragged him to the table, bent him over, ass up and dropped his pants. He kicked and struggled, but it was useless.

"Miss Toni, aim the camera at his face," Swag ordered, getting behind his bare ass.

She remembered Rain had the dick.

"Fuck! Lilly, gimme that pipe."

Lilly handed it to her. Swag slapped his ass.

"Damn, this shit jiggle." She laughed. "You got a fat one, nigguh!"

"Lights, camera, action!" Miss Toni sang, the phone aimed.

Tears ran down his cheeks. He gritted his teeth. But as soon as he felt the tip of the pipe, his mind hollered, "Diiiccckkkkk!" and he broke.

"Okay, okay! It always come in through the port!" he spat.

"When?" Swag probed, putting her finger right on his pucker.

"A week! A week maybe, a week and a half. You'll know when he move!"

Swag smiled at Miss Toni, then slapped his ass.

"Good girl!"

Now, tears poured from his eyes as he realized that he had broke and violated the code.

"What you waitin' for? Kill me, you faggot muhfucka! Kill me!" he cried.

Swag had mercy on him. She pulled out her .45 and clicked the safety off with her thumb.

"Like I said, last of a dying breed."

Bloc! Bloc! Bloc!

His brains spewed and splattered across the floor as his body collapsed, shook, then lay still forever. Swag tucked the gun.

"Get rid of him," she told the twins.

They immediately got busy. They dragged the body deep into the sewer, where the shrieks of the rats got more frantic, as if they were screaming, "Dinner! Dinner!"

Miss Toni laughed, shaking his head.

"Swag, you are cold-goddamn-blooded! How did you know that would break him?"

Swag shrugged.

"Take who somebody *thinks* they are, then show them who they really are," she explained.

"I gotta remember that . . . now that we know, are you sure this is what you want to do?"

"Definitely," Swag replied.

"This nigguh ain't Love," Miss Toni reminded her.

Swag smiled. "Scared?"

"Shitless," Miss Toni confessed.

They laughed.

"But I'm a loyal bitch, so I'm wit' you regardless. Just know, if you get us killed, I'ma beat yo' ass when we get to hell!" Miss Toni cackled.

"Trust me, baby, one by one all these nigguhs gonna fall. We'll own this city in twelve months," Swag replied confidently.

When she walked out, Miss Toni mumbled, "I hope so."

-4-

Rain woke up to Jazmine's tongue licking her pussy awake. When Jazmine got home, she found Rain sprawled out on the bed, on her back, dildo in her hand and passed out. Jazmine shed everything Swag-related on the floor and climbed up on the bed, putting Rain's legs over her shoulder, she feasted on her midnight snack.

"Ahh—" Rain gasped as she came to. "Ooh, Jazzzzz."

Rain loved the way Jazmine ate her pussy. She always knew when to apply pressure and when to let up. When to suck, where to lick, when to lick and where to suck. When to slide her fingers inside and massage her G-spot. And when to dart her lizard-like tongue in and out her asshole. Somehow Jazmine cracked the secret code to her deepest releases.

"Ahhhh, I'm 'bout to cummmmmm!" Rain squealed, trying to push Jazmine away and pull her closer at the same time.

She came thick and creamy, giving Jazmine another kind of moustache, one that after a deep, passionate kiss, they both wore.

"Damn, that was good," Rain snickered as she laid her eyes on Jazmine's breasts, fingering the locket in her cleavage.

"I wish we could lay like this forever," Jazmine fantasized, thinking about the plan that would either make her richer than she could ever imagine, or deader than she'd ever be.

Rain leaned up on her elbow and looked at her. "What are you thinking about?"

"Life."

Pause.

"You know I love you, right? I just . . . don't know how," Rain admitted.

Jazmine kissed her on the forehead. "With your heart."

Rain nodded, toying with the locket. She popped it open and looked at the picture inside, one Jazmine had shown her many times.

"Why don't you ever talk about him?" Rain asked.

Jazmine thought for a moment, shrugged and replied, "Because it's so . . . It's . . . bittersweet. And when I try or want to talk about him it sags on me like a heavy load."

"I understand. He was fine though."

Jazmine laughed, shaking her head. "Fine ain't the word. He was gorrrrgeous, and what used to make me so mad is he knew it too. Arrogant bastard."

Rain sat up and crossed her legs Indian style. "How did y'all meet?"

Jazmine hesitated a moment. Her past was too deep. She felt like: If she gazed upon the reflection of the waters of her memory, her reflection would reach up and pull her back under. But looking at Rain, she knew she was asking to let her in, and she wanted to, so she did . . . Even if it was only a glimpse.

"It happened on Bourbon Street . . . "

Mardi Gras also known as Fat Tuesday in English. Right before the holy season of Lent. The indulgence before austerity, the feast before the fast. It is the time when your every inner demon is given free rein, then you spend the rest of the year trying to bottle it back up. Bourbon Street. Beads. The fancy masks of the uninitiated. Children playing with fire. Dancing with the devil, everywhere the smell of lust, the look of desire, the addictive taste of sin . . .

He walked among the blissful throngs, his only mask, a smile. His one green eye and one gray eye made his reality seem surreal. Somewhere someone was playing "When the Saints Go Marching In" on a kazoo, a drunken slur of a song. Men in feathered plumes danced like they belonged in Congo square and breathed fire into the sky, to the squeamish delight of the tourists. Everywhere around, bare breasts hung, shook, and stood out. Firmly, beads proudly displayed, but none of it distracted him. He was focused on her . . . and him. Everything else was background noise. He liked the way she moved, the way she walked. Like she was a ballerina dancing through life, but slow enough for the rest of the world to keep up.

When he turned the corner, he caught a glimpse of her face, just enough to know he wanted to see more.

Focus . . . he reminded himself in Creole.

He checked his peripherals. The man had told his bodyguards to give him privacy, but they formed a loose ring that would contract like a boa if a problem arose. He was a problem waiting to happen. His eyes traveled over her shapely figure, her peach colored dress clinging to her scandalously, meshing nicely with her skin color. She had a body that was a sin to clothe. Part of him wanted to rip the dress from her body and make her walk naked through the streets to make her feel like she was making him feel.

Exposed.

But this was business.

Focus . . .

She knew he was there before she even saw him. Her sense of her surroundings was that of a wily survivor, that is to say, superb. She was like the gazelle that has survived for thousands of years around more powerful lions and vicious packs of hyenas, surviving only by its grace.

But when she looked into his eyes . . .

It happened as she and the man stepped into the hotel lobby. She turned. She saw. She froze. Caught. His verdant green eye like the lush comfort of a warm summer day. But his gray eye was as cold as a gray, rainy day, freezing as sleet. Caught. Between heaven and hell. Her only weapon was her smile, and she didn't hesitate to use it. Now they were even . . .

"Sir, the room is ready. It's been swept," one bodyguard reported.

"Good, good. Ah, just do what you do," he said, then looked her up and down. Admiringly. "I'm probably going to be awhile." He and the bodyguard shared a manly chuckle.

The prized possession sexily clung harder onto to his arm, admiring his physique. To her he was built like a NFL Linebacker. He had the right combination of

Chicago Cajun and Irish to make him one mean son of a bitch.

As soon as they went upstairs, turned the key, and entered the room, he pulled her to him aggressively.

"Baby, I hope you brought lunch, because this ol' Cajun is sho' long-winded." He chuckled.

She smiled and caressed his manhood through his trousers, but her mind warned, 'You'd better hurry . . . he's coming.'

##########

The building was only three stories. One of the many picturesque, old French styled buildings that the French Quarter is famous for. He surveyed the scene. One bodyguard in front of the building, one in the lobby. Another in the back staircase. But they were lax. The festivities of Mardi Gras had them in an indulgent mood. He wasn't, and often, moments like these came down to who wanted it more.

He entered through the kitchen. Later when questioned, the bus boy would say, "He . . . he moved like a shadow that spoke Creole. I don't know anything, I no want trouble!"

He used the dumb waiter to reach the top floor. The space inside the shaft was the square area of a chimney, big enough for him to fit, but small enough where he could wedge his back against one wall and plant his feet on the opposite wall. In this way he shimmied up three floors and crept out into the hallway. He quickly went out the hallway window, grabbing the ledge and pulling himself up onto the roof. Below him, the procession of the people partying, sacrificing themselves to an energy they didn't understand, an energy he possessed and therefore could rise above.

Literally.

He made his way along the roof, until he heard it. Her song. Her passionate moans floated out over the city as if the soundtrack to the debauchery below. It was a song he promised himself she would soon sing to him, and then he'd punish her for eternity, for singing it to another man.

Gripping the edge of the roof, he slowly and as quietly as a cat, lowered himself to the balcony below. He pulled out the twin .45 chromes, reflecting the wickedness in the moon's glow. Silently, he stepped into the room. She was riding him. Her body rolling like a melody rides a rhythm. Her bare back flexing and incensing, head thrown back, her song aimed at heaven. He aimed the gun. Usually, he'd fire once, then she'd slump, twice, thrice and his body would explode, slow and spasm. But he hesitated. The man on the bed opened his eyes and sat up. He saw the gleam, gasped, hugged her to him as a shield . . . or so he thought.

Pfffzzzt! Pfffzzzt!

He was an excellent marksman. He shot over her shoulder right into his right eye, blowing pupil, cornea and retina all over her neck and chin. The second shot made his brains dive out the back of his head and splatter all over the wall as if his brain cells had found an escape. The big man cried out and slumped. He aimed the gun at her.

"Turn around," he hissed in Creole.

"Are you going to kill me?" she responded in Creole.

"Turn around," he gritted.

She did, her luscious body glistened with the sweat of her fragrance.

"Don't . . . kill me."

"You are a thief. Give it back," he demanded.

"I—I don't know what you're talking about," her tone said, but her eyes betrayed her.

His bodyguard had heard the cry. He knew it wasn't sex. He knocked hard.

"Boss! Boss, you okay?"

She glared at the gunman with a gaze that screamed, go! Get out of here now!

Deep down, he knew he should kill her, kill her before . . .

The door splintered as the burly bodyguard kicked it in. He reached for his gun, while yelling, "Boss is hit!"

Ppffffzzzzt!

One shot through the head toppled him dead. He aimed at her as he backed out on to the balcony. Then he tucked the guns and pulled himself out of sight. Two more bodyguards rushed into the room.

"He's on the roof! He's on the roof!" one man barked, catching a glimpse of his foot disappearing up.

He fired into the night, uselessly, feeling like he had to do something. The dead man's bodygaurds swarmed from everywhere. She wrapped the sheet around her, listening to the cacophony of voices swirling around her.

"He's on the roof!"

"No, he's gone!"

"He can't be!"

"Where is he?"

"He disappeared!"

"Nobody disappears!"

But she knew he had, but she also knew that she would see him again . . .

-5-

The waitress was beautiful. She looked like Jennifer Lopez in her prime. Young, nubile Latino girl, the short restaurant skirt revealing her long, sexy brown legs.

Every time she came by, he smiled. She smiled back. He knew he was in; he wouldn't tug the line too hard. The trap was already set.

"More coffee?" she asked, smile beaming.

"As long as you're the one pouring," he flirted, purposely being corny but sweet because sincerity is seldom smooth.

She smiled. This was the second day he had come into the restaurant, but the day before he hadn't spoken. He only focused on his laptop, effectively ignoring her. She liked his freckles. She had never known an albino, but because he was so fine, she wondered what a snow-white dick would look like.

"You're very pretty, Carmen," he said, as if reading her name tag.

She blushed. "Thank you."

"I just had to say it. Now a days, everyone seems scared to give a compliment. Like it's going to cost them an arm and a leg. People spend so much time focusing in on the negative. I for one, would rather focus on the beauty in the world, you know?" he expressed.

"I–I agree. Umm, anything else?"

"No. I'm good."

Reluctantly, she walked away.

When she brought the bill, he put two one-hundred-dollar bills on the table.

"What's that?" Carmen questioned.

"Your tip." He smiled charmingly.

Her eyes swelled as if she'd hit the lottery.

"Oh my . . . thank you."

He shrugged like the nothing it was.

"I can tell this is just a steppingstone for you. You look like the type destined for big things. Are you going to school?"

"Actually, I am."

"What for?"

"Financial management."

He chuckled.

"What a coincidence," he remarked, removing a card from his pocket and handing it to her. "I'm a Fund Manager with Pimco."

Her eyes glossed as she read the card:

Pimco Fund

Steven Natas

555 – 6874

Pimco was one of the biggest bond dealers in the world. She had applied for an internship there. Of course, he knew that. He knew everything about her. He had used his phone's facial recognition software to scan her face the day before. Several seconds later, her name popped up, along with her social media network. He knew she was in school, knew her Pimco internship dream job, her favorite color and her favorite song. Everything he needed to create coincidences.

"Wow, I applied for an internship. I'm still waiting to hear something," she replied.

"Well, I can't make you any promises. After all, just because you're pretty doesn't mean you're smart." He chuckled. "But if you jot down our full name and number down on something, I'll check with HR for you. You know, check the status."

"Would you?" She gasped. "That would be great."

"No problem . . . listen, when do you get off? Why don't I take you home? My limo's right outside."

"Actually, my boyfriend usually picks me up. He'll be here in a few minutes," she replied with subtle reluctance.

As if Satan didn't already know . . .

He smiled knowingly and replied, "Carmen, it's a cold world. You don't need a boy, you need a man, but I can still be the friend part, too . . . I'm not suggesting we elope—I'm offering a ride. *You* determine the destination."

At that point she stopped thinking and started feeling. He was gorgeous, rich, and offering a ride into her future. Her beating . . . beating . . . feeling . . . cheating heart sighed and swallowed the hook. Had she stayed true to her boyfriend, who was saving up to buy her a wedding ring, I wouldn't be telling her story now. But she wanted her cake and to eat it, too. Thinking, *who would know?*

Nobody would *ever* . . . know.

"I'll wait."

She went. She came. They left. The driver opened the door. Satan and Carmen stepped in. They drove off.

"What is this?" she asked, looking around the luxurious interior.

"A stretch Rolls Royce," he replied, as if bored with the question.

"It's beautiful." She gawked.

He caressed her cheek. "Not as beautiful as you."

She smiled, but his lengthy nails, although manicured to perfection, made her move away slightly.

"I told you, I have a boy—a man," she reminded him, with the tease evident in her voice.

He chuckled. "I suppose this is the part where I'm supposed to chase you, but that would be silly, since you belong to me," he reasoned.

The friendly smile on her face melted.

"I don't belong to anyone," she replied, feeling the change in the vibe like somebody had opened the freezer door on her life. "Maybe this was a mistake. Take me back to my job."

Satan crossed his legs, brushed imaginary lint from his pants and said, "I'm taking you to your new job."

Reality slapped her in the face.

"Stop the car! Stop this fuckin' car!" she yelled, then tried the door handle, only to find it irrevocably locked.

Satan hit a button and black partitions slid over the windows making it impossible to see in.

"Did you hear me? I said stop this fuckin—" was all she got out, before the ringing in her ears from the vicious backhand made it seem like she was spinning in place.

Calmly, he rubbed her leg as she slumped in the corner, holding her bloody lip and looking at him in abject horror.

"You brought that on yourself. Now, if that's what you're into . . . I'll do it again," he explained, looking at her coldly.

Tears ran down her cheek.

"Please . . . I have a little girl."

"How old is she?" Satan asked with such interest, she knew not to say anything.

"Now . . . take off your clothes."

She didn't move.

"I . . . will do it again," he reminded her.

With trembling hands, she stripped down to her soft, brown freckled skin, revealing curves like a coke bottle. He ran his eyes over her body lustfully.

"Nice . . . you'll do well. Now, suck my dick."

-6-

Boom! Shick-Shack! Boom!

"Everybody! Get down on the ground now!" the gunman in the Richard Nixon mask bellowed, working in the stock of the riot pump shotgun and letting off two slugs into the ceiling.

It had all happened so fast.

One minute the late morning crowd was ordering an early lunch, giving Kingfish's restaurant a steady buzz of building voices. Then they came swarming through the front and the kitchen at the same time. Twelve in number, all armed and masked with the faces of ex-presidents: Bush, Nixon, Clinton, three Reagans, three Lincolns, and two Roosevelts, Teddy and Franklin. They quickly herded the kitchen workers into the dining area to join the patrons on the floor. The only man standing was a furious Kingfish, behind the counter.

"I said on the floor, fat ass nigguh!" Nixon barked, his riot pump inches from Kingfish's nose.

"Fuck you!" Kingfish seethed.

Shick–shack!

"Relax, yo. He's the man I came to see," said the Obama masked man strolling through the door. "Collect *all* the phones and snatch the surveillance tape," he ordered. Gun in hand.

Obama bopped up to the counter and slid onto the stool in front of Kingfish on the other side of the counter. In front of him was a hot plate of chicken gizzards, a bottle of hot sauce, and an unopened coke.

"Damn yo, I love gizzards. You mind?" Obama aimed to annoy Kingfish, sliding the plate over.

Kingfish was so mad, he was trembling, but the chrome in Obama's hand looked hungry to speak.

Swag slid the Obama mask to the top of her head, chewing a gizzard.

"Yeah, Fish, you a beast in that kitchen." Swag chuckled.

"You know who I am?" Kingfish growled.

"Do you know who *I* am?" Swag shot right back. "We haven't been properly introduced. I'm your new partner, and they call me Swag."

Kingfish stared at Swag's face, wondering where he had seen him before. Suddenly, Swag jumped up and slapped him with the pistol, staggering Kingfish, then slammed his face into the counter and put the gun to the back of his head.

"It ain't polite to stare, you fat piece of shit," Swag growled.

Swag knew it was never good to let someone who knew both her sides to stare long. What the eye doesn't see, the mind can. Now, with a face full of countertop, his mind was focused on pain.

"Nigguh, you better kill me, because you can't extort me. I ain't Love!" Kingfish fumed.

"Oh, so you *do* know me. That's good, because now we can cut to the chase. If I don't eat, *you* don't eat, ya heard? I don't play no fuckin' games, believe me. Ask your nephew. When's the last time you heard from him?" Swag was being a wiseass.

Right then Kingfish knew why he couldn't get in touch with his nephew. He had been calling and texting him for three days. The last time he heard from him, he was supposed to be meeting Miss Toni. An angry tear snaked the length of his flared nostril and fell on the counter.

"You goddamn son of a—" Kingfish began to spit.

Swag brought the gun down hard on his nose, breaking it instantly, then slammed his face into the counter again. Kingfish's head exploded with pain. Swag leaned in close to his ear and said, "Yeah, I see you understand. He dead. I killed him, then I fed him to the rats. Right now, they probably shitting his remains all over the sewer." He laughed. "But before I killed him, I fucked him in the ass. He loved it. You could say he died a new man. Almost like being born again, but in reverse."

Kingfish loved his nephew like a son because he didn't have one. The pain in his face was nothing compared to what he felt in his heart. A part of him wanted to try for Swag's gun, to either kill or be killed. The other part of him wasn't sure if he was ready to die trying. So, he ate his anger, hopefully to shit it on Swag someday real soon.

"What do you want?" Kingfish gritted.

"Money and product. Every week. I'ma let you determine the amount just to see if you'd try and disrespect me. Remember, I got a small army to feed, so don't be a Jew. If I feel disrespected by your offering, I will burn this place to the ground, and everywhere you plant a seed, I'll kill it before it *grows*. Are we clear?" Swag barked.

"Yeah," Kingfish mumbled.

"Good, 'cause I don't repeat myself. Don't play with me, Kingfish, because if you do, when I come for you . . . I'ma fuck you, too, and with all that ass, I might just like it." Swag chuckled, then kissed his temple.

He brought the gun down hard at the base of Kingfish's skull knocking him out instantly. His enormous body crashed to the floor like a harpooned walrus.

Swag grabbed the plate of gizzards and the hot sauce. He turned to one of the Reagans.

"Pull his pants down and leave 'em around his ankles. When he wakes up, he'll be scared to death." Swag laughed, and the rest of the presidents joined him.

Reagan number two Kingfish's pants down, then they walked out leaving Kingfish assed out . . . literally.

-7-

"And guess who has been off the radar?" Gloria, Rain's hairdresser, began her conversation with Rain in her styling chair.

"Who?" Rain asked, all ears.

She had been out of the loop for so long, she needed to catch up on *The Hood Tea* . . .

"Tosha."

"Tosha? Light-skin Tosha? Schemin' ass Tosha?"

Gloria nodded.

"Mm–hmm. Tosha. You know ever since Mona got killed, she been actin' like she Queen Hi-Yellow."

Rain smirked to herself. She knew all about Mona's death. She was still upset she wasn't the cause.

"So what? She found a trick or somethin'?"

"Don't nobody know. They saw her leave wit' some fine ass albino nigguh in a stretch Rolls Royce, and she ain't been around since," Gloria blabbed.

"Shit, a stretch Rolls? I get in something like that, you won't see me no more either." Rain laughed.

They both laughed.

"I know that's right. And speakin' of you, Miss Thing, you ain't been on the radar yourself. What you got goin' on?" Gloria inquired.

"Damn, nosy."

"Bitch, please. Don't even act like you ain't all up in people bidness; this time it just happens to be yours," Gloria cracked.

"Just bein' a mommy, thinkin' about goin' back to school," Rain hinted.

"Mm–hmm. Girl, you know if anybody know you, I know you, and you can't sleep if you ain't got an iron in the fire somewhere!"

Rain could just hear Gloria talking to the next bitch, "Yeah, you know Rain—blah blah blah . . ."

So, she wasn't about to feed into it.

Forty minutes later, she walked out, hair did, fresh to death and feeling like her period was on its way, because she was craving chocolate.

She thought she remembered having had a mini Snickers for Malaya in her purse, so she looked, hoping it was still there. She had her head down, nose in her purse looking for chocolate. As she walked out the door, she felt herself bump into a solid body.

"Oh, excuse me!"

Looking for chocolate? Hello chocolate . . .

He was dark chocolate. Wesley Snipes dark chocolate. Tall enough to block the glare of the sun as she looked up into his chinky brown eyes. He was dressed for success, suited, conservative cut, tastefully understated and a soft warm smile that she could tell she was the cause for.

"Don't—don't worry about—I wasn't looking . . ." Rain semi-stammered.

He chuckled and held up his iPhone.

"Neither was I. Candy Crush," he admitted.

They shared a self-conscious chuckle to avoid the chemistry evident in the air.

"I'm sure you're in a hurry, so . . ." he implied, stepping out of her way.

"No, no, I was just . . . looking for some chocolate," she replied, keeping the flirt out of her tone, because the words were enough.

His smile said 'message received.'

"Well, there is a Starbucks not far from here. Chocolate's on me?" he suggested, throwing the ball back into her court.

Rain sneered. "I don't drink with strangers."

"Oh, I'm sorry. I'm Tony. Tony Matson."

"Rain," she replied, seduction dripping from her thick lips.

The conversation flowed smoothly as Matson and Rain enjoyed lattes and laughter. She thought their meeting was confidential. He knew better.

He had convinced himself that he was doing it to get at Jazmine. That he was doing it because he needed to get in the house and put a GPS chip on that bike. His gut told him she used the bike to do her dirt. He didn't know how right he was. Matson had put the name Swag in the police computer. It came back with more questions than answers . . .

Michael Jean

He knew the last name was pronounced like John. It was French, by way of Haiti.

AKA Gaws/ AKA Swag

Gaws . . . Gaws . . . Gaws, the name echoed in his head until he realized why. It was Swag backwards. He smiled. Swag both ways . . .

All of his charges were in Louisiana: New Orleans, Baton Rouge, Shreveport. Robbery, murder, murder, murder, murder . . . seven in all. But what caught Matson's eye was he had beaten *every* charge! Seven murder charges, seven acquittals. He knew Louisiana used a different type of legal system, but *no one* could beat that many charges without a heavy hand to tip the scales of justice.

"Who do you know?" Matson had asked the mug shot on the screen.

Deceased.

"Deceased?" Matson echoed.

He read that he was killed in his city. In fact, Matson remembered the case. It was a cold case. No leads. He was found in his own blood. It had been phoned in by an anonymous tip.

Was it a female? he thought.

He could go back and check the G.H. report. Matter of fact . . . he headed down into the bowels of the station where cold case files were stored, gathering dust until hunches like the one Matson was following came along.

He pulled the box down. There wasn't much physical evidence. He checked the report and saw that the anonymous tipster was believed to be a female.

And there was something else feminine in the box.

A footprint.

Tiny. A size five. Whoever it was, she had stepped in the blood that pooled around his cold body.

The killer?

Initially they had thought so because the closet was filled with women's clothes and shoes. Size five. But the trajectory of the bullet came from someone at least six feet tall. If she was involved, she definitely wasn't the shooter. But she was never found.

Was she Rain?

"Swag," she had gasped, lips parted, pussy creaming all over Matson's thoughts.

Focus . . .

"Size five," he mumbled to himself.

And so Operation Cinderella was born.

It wasn't an official investigation. It was personal. Very personal, as personal as his hatred for Jazmine, as personal as his fetish for that perfectly arched foot leaving prints all over his lust.

Very personal . . .

"I wonder . . ." he mumbled to himself.

Size five. His mind convinced his lower self that they only wanted to see the shoe size . . . and not the foot itself.

He followed her to the salon and waited. A part of him knew this wasn't the way to go about an official investigation, but he felt he had good intentions.

The road to hell is paved with good intentions. He was well on his way.

"Oh, excuse me!" he had said, as if it were all a mistake.

. . . It was . . .

"I like your shoes," he remarked, as they sat sipping.

"Oh!" She put out her foot, turning it so he could see every angle. "Ruthie Davis; I love her work."

His eyes fixed on the delicious appeal of her French pedicure. He couldn't help but wonder how it tasted.

"They love you too." He smiled.

She blushed, then looked him in the eyes and remarked, "I notice you're wearing a ring."

It wasn't just a random comment. It was a line in the sand, one that Matson didn't hesitate to cross because he convinced himself he wasn't crossing it.

"Does that bother you?"

"No," she replied, looking him straight in the eyes. Her gaze said, "Now we both know exactly why we're here. Looking for chocolate . . ."

Before he could reply, his phone rang.

"Yeah," he answered. ". . . okay, I'm on my way." He hung up. "Listen, gorgeous, I have to go. Do you think I could—"

She didn't let him finish. She smoothly removed the phone from his hand, put in her number, then pressed send. When her phone rang, she handed his back.

"It's for you." She smirked seductively.

He took it. She picked up her purse and latte and started to walk off, then turned and said, "Aren't you going to answer?"

She went out the door. He answered.

"Hello?"

"I think you are very sexy, and I look forward to seeing you again very soon," Rain purred.

Just picturing her lips saying those words made him hard. He was so busy picturing her naked he almost forgot about the other naked woman on his mind.

The one dead in the middle of the street.

-8-

Two goons.

They were only two goons looking to come up in Satan's organization. They knew the quickest way to be noticed was by bringing in choice pieces that brought the boss a lot of money. So, when they saw her, they *knew* she was a choice piece.

"She so white," the one called Black remarked.

"She so clean," the one called Blue replied.

She combined the best of both worlds. The golden blonde hair and sky-blue eyes of a white girl, with the tiny waist, curvaceous hips, and bodacious ass of the blackest black girl. She was walking through the mall with two light-skinned, equally gorgeous, black girls, but they paled in comparison to the milky white of the choice piece. She looked like Ice T's wife Coco, and they had to have her.

"Yo, the boss *never* gets his hands on no white girls, so I *know* he gonna love her," Blue assumed.

And without further conversation, they made their move. It didn't take much convincing. They were both holding lots of Dolla, a mouthful of gold teeth, a strong 'N'awlins accent, and Coco just loooooved Lil' Wayne. Ten minutes later, the two goons and three chicks were on the way to the room.

Ffwock! went the cork of the bubbling bubbly.

Fffffffff! went the inhalation of the exotic blended blunt.

Gulp! went the swallowed molly.

Giggle, giggle, touch, touch . . . "Let me see y'all kiss. . ."

Muah! Got muffled into mmmmmm, and clothes were shed like leaves in the fall . . .

"Ohhhh fuckkk . . ." Five naked bodies forming a drunken daisy chained orgy until . . .

"Aarrgghh!"

"No, please stop!"

"Help!"

"Bitch, shut up!"

Blood curdling screams . . .

Wire hangers twisted up into what is known by the initiated as a pimp stick, can make a bitch leap five feet off the floor and cling to the ceiling like a scared cat, and then beat her back down again.

"Get—" Blue huffed, out of breath. "Get the brand."

At his feet lay all three chicks, beaten, bruised, and bloody. Black got out the brand and cut it on. They rolled all three chicks on their stomachs.

"Why . . . why are you doing—" Coco mumbled through purple lips.

Smack!

"Bitch shut up!"

Sssssssssssssssssssss!

When the sizzle of the double dragon branded on to Coco's ass, Black muffled her agonized screech with a pillow. The next two screamed just as helplessly, especially when the alcohol felt like red ants tearing through the burn.

Several more blows and the chicks were as pliant as lifeless bodies. Black and Blue wrapped a sheet over Coco then dumped her in the van. Blue stayed with Coco while Black went back in and got one of the red-bones. The last red-bone lay on the carpet knowing this was her last chance. She fought the urge to just jump up and run because she didn't know where Blue had actually gone. So she waited. Waited until Black wrapped the sheet around her, picked her up and carried her out. She cracked one eye and saw Blue standing by the sliding van door. She knew if they put her in the van, she'd never see her mama again. She wasn't about to let that happen.

"Aaaaaaagh fuck!" Black cried as she sank her teeth into his cheek so hard she drew blood.

He instantly let her go. As soon as her feet hit the ground, they were already running.

"She gettin' away!" Blue yelled.

He didn't move because he didn't want the two in the van to get away. Two in the hand is better than one on foot.

But Black took off like a bolt behind her. He was gonna kick a bone out her ass. She dashed straight into the street, not looking, not caring. The sound of her heartbeat in her ears drowned out the blare of the SUV's horn.

Skrrrreeeech!

The driver slammed on the brakes, but it was too late. The impact, the sickening thud, the crunch of human bone against industry steel and she was airborne.

It hurt so bad that her conscious was fading fast. Her soul told her it would never return. The embrace of death saddened her, but one thought made her soul smile as it left her body. The thought that, though she would never see her mother again, her mother would see her again, and she would know she had died fighting.

By the time her body hit the ground twenty feet away, that was all it was. A body.

"Yo, let's go!" Blue yelled.

The driver of the SUV looked at Black. Black backpedaled, then went and jumped in the van. They skidded off, leaving out the alternate exit.

##########

Matson and Jazmine arrived at the scene about the same time. Across the street, a large crowd, held back by crime scene tape and a monitoring officer, gawked. TV news cameras lined the press area set up in the motel parking lot, while several reporters gave on the spot coverage. Police milled around and forensics marked and analyzed everything. The star of the show lay in the middle of the street under a bloody sheet.

"Glad to see you've got time in your busy schedule to do your job," Matson bitched. Not hiding how bitter he was towards Jazmine as she made her approach.

Ducking under the tape, she draped her detective shield over her neck. It bounced against the bulletproof vest she wore over her clothes. "And what's that supposed to mean, Matson?" Jazmine shot back.

He shrugged. "Just letting you know I recognize how . . . busy you are!"

Jazmine always sought peace before war, but he was pushing it.

"Matson, do you have something against me?"

"Not something, *everything*. I know you were the one behind that bullshit at my house, not to mention Hall . . . so just know, Coleman, I *don't* forget," Matson seethed.

They glared at each other. The hate was palpable.

"If you two turtle doves are through cooing, how about we get on this case," Chief Jordan remarked as he walked up.

Reluctantly, they both turned to him.

"What do we know, Chief?" Matson asked

"Not much. But hopefully enough. The guy that hit her says she was running from some guy. Dark skinned with—get this—a bleeding cheek . . . Anyway, the vic runs out in the street and boom! Impact throws her like a rag doll. End of story."

"Any lead on *why* he was chasing her?" Jazmine wanted to know.

Jordan nodded toward the open motel room door where forensics was busy at work.

"Apparently they were in that room. We found blood and semen in there, everywhere. Plus, a bloody braided wire . . . contraption. Looks like the perp beat her with it."

"Then I guess we can assume at some point she bit him on the cheek and took off." Jazmine looked out at the body. "I need to see her."

"Be my guest. Both of you. Matson, we found several pills and what appears to be marijuana. The drugs are your jurisdiction. Coleman, the murder's yours. Both of you say hello to your new partner." Jordan chuckled, knowing there was bad blood. He added, "And if you do kill each other, do it after we solve the case. So, you kids have fun." Jordan walked away.

Matson and Jazmine moved towards the body. A female from forensics with a camera was taking pictures of the area around the body. She looked up.

"Hello, detectives, I'm glad you're here. I found something I think you should see," the woman from forensics said. She squatted down and pulled up the sheet. The girl's body was twisted in a grotesque angle, almost like an action figure whose bottom half was facing the same way as the top half, only in the opposite direction.

Her torso faced up and so did her ass.

But it wasn't the unnatural contortion of death that chilled Jazmine's blood in her veins. Pulling back the sheet on the body made her gasp like someone had pulled back the one over her past.

It was the double dragons . . .

They seemed to sing, "I'm baaaaaaaackkk!"

The voice in her head spoke so loudly it seemed to come from everywhere. She looked up, expecting to see the face so much that she saw it . . . in the back of the crowd . . . in the back of a police car . . . standing in the parking lot. That face that she knew well.

The Albino . . .

The one with the eyes that always glowed red in every picture he ever took. He said it was only the optics of the flash, but she knew it wasn't because he was exactly who he said he was . . .

Satan.

"Just relax, baby. This won't hurt . . . much. Be a big girl for daddy, okay?" he urged, voice soft and deceptively silky.

"Okay, daddy."

Sssssssssssssssss!

The sizzle seemed to go to the bone, but she sucked in her breath and refused to cry out. She didn't want to disappoint him.

Coleman . . .

Coleman . . .

"Coleman," Matson called her three times in total before she blinked back to reality.

She was so discombobulated, her mask so out of place that she inadvertently replied in French, "Je ne regretted rien. . ."

"What did you say?" Matson questioned, vaguely making it out above her mumble.

"No–nothing. I'm okay," she replied, before turning to walk away.

Matson sensed a connection between Jazmine and the brand. He had seen the way her eyes glazed over when the sheet was pulled back. It was obvious that it was familiar to her, and he was determined to find out why.

"Make sure I get a picture of that ASAP," Matson told forensics, before turning to catch up with Jazmine.

"So, what do you think?" he asked her.

"I–umm–I don't know. I have to go. I'm going to . . . wait on the lab reports," she answered, but he could tell the words were nothing but words. He had never seen her so distracted, and a part of him, the part he tried to hide even from himself, was enjoying seeing her so fucked up after knowing her as a cold, calculating bitch. She truly looked like she had seen a ghost.

"Yeah, you do that," he mumbled to himself, watching her drive away.

-9-

"What do you think about a threesome?"

Those were the first words Jazmine heard when she walked into her condo, as if Rain couldn't wait for her to get home.

By that time, Jazmine's composure was beginning to return, and her conniving mind was once again whirling. He was here. That was obvious. But she felt like she had the upper hand.

Swag.

She looked at Rain.

"With who?"

"Baby, I'm tellin' you—this nigguh is foine! Wesley Snipes in *New Jack City* foine!" Rain giggled like the thought was delicious.

"What's his name?" Jazmine asked.

"Tony. I met him at the salon. He's married, but fuck that. I don't want him. I just want some dick. I got a man." She winked, wrapping her arms around Jazmine's neck and kissing her.

"Shit, I need some too." Jazmine chuckled. "Set it up."

"You okay?"

"Why you ask?"

"Because you're usually so paranoid about who you let in the circle. Now, it's like, set it up," Rain remarked.

Jazmine smiled, looked her in the eyes, and replied, "I trust you."

The sentiment made Rain mist up.

"I'm glad . . . Now, when are you going to tell me the rest of the story?"

Jazmine went in the refrigerator for a carrot.

"What story?"

"Swag!" Rain replied, like duh! "You fell asleep, remember? I wanna know why he ain't shoot you. Where he go? Did you see him again? Tell me," she whined, as if fiending for the ending of a juicy novel.

Jazmine chuckled. Just thinking of Swag made her feel warm. Protected. And at that moment, she needed to feel all the protection she could get . . .

##########

When he walked into the church, she was surprised he didn't burst into flames, because his smirk was so wicked, his intentions had to be.

She had just stood up in a choir robe to sing "His Eye is on the Sparrow" . . . but her soul fluttered away, leaving her voice slightly off key as he aimed his gaze dead at her, and its heat felt like the beam of an infrared.

He smiled and swaggered his way to the front row, knowing exactly what he was doing to her, knowing his eyes had her voice by the throat, enjoying it and only relenting when he sat down and looked at the preacher on his throne, who had been watching him like a hawk the whole time. He nodded subtly. Swag nodded back. She cleared her throat, shut her eyes to make it better, but it only made it worse . . . green and gray . . . and sang angelically.

She knew he was looking at her. She could feel his eyes all over her, picturing her body naked under the choir robe, picturing her singing another kind of song, the one that came from deeper down. The thought made her wet, made her imagine him ripping the hypocrisy of the cross-covered choir robe from her body and exposing her throbbing flesh underneath.

She wasn't the only one who felt it. The congregation felt it; they just didn't know what they were feeling as the sixteen-year-old songstress rendered a very different version of a very old hymn. But they felt it through her song. No one had ever sung "The Sparrow" like . . . that. The way her voice fluttered, dipped, groaned . . . yearned. It made the gospel sound as erotic as the Songs of Solomon, if sung.

"Jesus . . ." a woman whispered feverishly, squirming in the pew, grabbing and squeezing her husband's hand.

When she finished, the silence was loud. There were no amens, no hallelujahs, just awkward, uncomfortable silence. The preacher stood up, cleared his throat, and approached the pulpit.

"Yes, yes, praise . . . God." He smirked, looking out over his large congregation. "Can I get an amen?"

". . . Amen," the congregation said with hesitation.

"Amen," he repeated, raising his voice an octave.

"Amen," they thundered.

"Amen." He nodded. "Now at this time, is there anyone who wants to be prayed for, who wants to be saved today, who wants the light . . . the light of the mornin', yes, the morning light (Isaiah 14:12 and Revelation 22:16) in their lives, come on down this morning!" he urged.

"Praise the Lord!"

"Yessss!"

"I hear you, Lord!"

A mother approached with her twelve-year-old daughter, but so did a young girl of twenty-three and a woman of thirty. All came down the aisle, right hands held high, high heels caressing the carpet with graceful strides and open hearts as they approached the front.

Swag took it all in with a detached amusement. He turned his attention to her. She was watching him. This time, unafraid. Acclimated. He got up to approach her but felt a hand on his shoulder as he turned. He turned back.

It was the preacher.

"I'm glad you could make it," the preacher remarked in French.

Swag nodded.

"Oui."

They shook hands. The pastor had a strong grip, his coal black eyes never letting go of Swag's. His snow-white alabaster skin, a stark contrast to the severe black suit the Albino wore.

"Aria . . . Aria. Come here," he called out.

Several people came and shook the pastor's hand, congratulating him on the service until Aria finally arrived.

"Swag, I'm sure you and my daughter have already met." He smirked knowingly.

Swag nodded.

"In passing," he replied in Creole, the language he always spoke, although he knew English.

"I'm sure . . . Aria, take these sisters in the back. I'll be there shortly," the pastor instructed.

"Okay, Daddy," she smiled, turning to the women who wanted to be . . . saved.

"Come. We can talk in my office."

When they reached his office, the pastor shut the door behind them. Although he called it an office, it was more like a study. Bookshelves made of cherry oak lined two walls. A third had a bar. In the corner was a love seat and an armchair. Swag sat in the armchair. The pastor went to the bar.

"I assume Bourbon will do?"

Swag nodded, shrugged.

He handed Swag his glass, then took a book from the shelf and handed it to him too, as he took his seat.

Swag looked at the book with a frown.

"I can't read."

"Can you count?" The pastor chuckled, then sipped his Bourbon.

Swag caught on. He opened the book. Inside, the book was hollowed out and filled with a stack of money. Swag started to take the money out.

"Keep the book, too. Can't have you walking out of here with a handful of Dolla."

Swag set the book beside him.

"Satan, I—"

The pastor shook his head.

"Around here I'm known as Pastor . . . just a simple Parrish pastor." He winked. "Do you know who it was you killed?"

"I don't want to know," Swag replied.

"You need to . . . so please, humor me. He was a State Senator. Bought and paid for, but he was dishonest. He wouldn't stay bought."

Swag laughed softly.

"You see. There is no one in Louisiana I cannot touch. I'm getting ready to make a major move. I want you to work for me. I will give you control over any ward you want," Satan offered.

Swag smiled to himself. He knew why Satan wanted him to know what the hit was. He wanted to show him his power, then offer him control, when in actuality he was taking control.

"I work better alone. I do the job. No more, no?"

Satan studied Swag over the rim of his glass. He had used him many times, but he was becoming a power in his own right. Quietly, like a whisper on the wind Satan couldn't ignore. Usually, people like that he simply crushed. But, one thing stood in his way.

"How is the old woman?"

Swag looked at him evenly.

"She . . . is . . ."

Satan nodded. Downed his drink, then set the glass down with finality and stood up.

"Very good. I will be in touch," he said, holding out his hand.

Swag stood and shook it.

"You know how to find me."

"And remember, my offer stands open . . . but that is all I'm offering," Satan warned.

Swag understood instantly. He may not have been able to read words, but he could read eyes.

Stay away from her . . .

##########

He came to her later in her room. She knew he would.

"He . . . saw you at the hotel?" Satan questioned.

"It all happened so fast, there was no time," Aria lied, avoiding his gaze.

"Come here."

She looked up, then crossed the room to him. She was in the middle of taking off the dress she had worn to church. She had already unzipped the back so the top half folded and fell on top of the bottom half revealing her black, lace bra.

He kissed her forehead . . . then her lips, while simultaneously slipping his hand in her stockings, past her panties, and caressed the lips of her pussy. Her juices dripped into his hand like honey dew from a melon.

He smiled.

"All this for me?"

Aria reached to wrap her arms around his neck.

"Always."

Satan caressed her cheek with his long, manicured nails.

"I taught you a lot . . . but not enough to lie to me."

"I—"

He seized her throat with the grip of a python, one massive hand wrapped around her neck.

"Stay. Away. From. Him," he seethed through gritted teeth.

His grip was so tight; she instantly got lightheaded.

"I haven't done anything!"

"Stay away!" he roared, then his face broke into a wicked grin. "Maybe . . . it's time I paid your mother a visit."

The fear in her eyes seemed to stiffen her whole body throughout.

"No . . . I won't disobey you."

He relaxed his grip.

"Get on your knees," he demanded calmly.

She sank without hesitation, unbuckling his pants and pulling out his thick rod. When she took him into her mouth, he threw his head back, enthralled, because total control over a person is . . . heavenly.

-10-

Satan paced the floor. Thirty of his golden toothed goons stood around the room damn near at attention. Nobody spoke. Nigguhs took turns breathing, so as not to rustle up the wind. They were so scared, there wasn't an unclenched asshole among them.

Blue and Black stood in the middle.

"Boss, I swear we–we . . . man, she was so *beautiful*, we *knew* you'd get a lot of money for the bitch!" Black tried to reason.

Satan stopped pacing. His back to them.

"Beautiful? Tell me . . . have you ever known me to procure a white bitch?"

"No, but—"

Satan turned and his expression silenced them.

"Do you know why? Do you? Because if word got out that I had white pussy, the Feds would be all over me, Interpol would be all over me, and I would lose *everything* behind one. White. Bitch! That's why! Nobody gives a fuck about Black bitches, Latinas, and Asians. Do you understand?"

They both nodded vigorously.

"Say it then. Who do we snatch?"

"Black bitches, Latinas, and Asians," they replied in broken unison.

"Again!"

"Black bitches, Latinas, and Asians!"

"Again!"

He had them repeat it over and over again so they would remember it for the rest of their lives . . . literally.

Boc! Boc!

Satan pulled out the nine and head checked Black then Blue with a single dome shot apiece. Then turned to the rest of the goons.

"Any questions?"

Not a one . . .

"Dump 'em with the white girl. Nobody cares about a dead white bitch found with two nigguhs. They'll say she deserved it," Satan spat then walked out.

##########

Jazmine pulled up to Kingfish's restaurant and went inside. It was late afternoon, so the place wasn't as packed. Besides, the incident a few days earlier had people a little leery.

She walked in and headed straight for his office, then knocked on the closed door.

"Come in!" Kingfish yelled out.

She entered to find him doing what he did best. Eating. Chicken gizzards. Always the country gentleman, he was quick to oblige, "Have some."

"Gizzards? I never touch 'em." She smirked as she sat down, then cut straight to the chase. "So, what happened?"

"What happened is right! I called you two-goddamn-days ago! What the fuck took you so long?"

Jazmine eyed her press on nails and replied, "Kingfish, I'm not one of your flunkies. I was busy. You and I have *an* arrangement, not my *only* arrangement. You want to be more of a priority, make me a better offer."

He grumbled, drowned his gizzards in more hot sauce then gulped his beer.

"Who the fuck is Swag?"

"Swag?"

"Yeah, *Swag.*"

Jazmine shrugged before she answered. "Some thug. He tried to extort Love. I'm not sure if he was successful, but he did 'cause him a lot of headaches. Why?"

"Because that's the sum bitch come bustin' up in here! He's trying to extort me! Me! So, I want to know who the fuck he is!" Kingfish ranted, veins popping, looking one gizzard away from a heart attack.

"With a team like yours, you can't find out?"

He shook his head. "Nobody knows nothin', and if they do, the streets ain't talkin'. He's like a fuckin' . . . *ghost*."

Or a woman, Jazmine mused to herself.

"You ask Miss Toni?"

"Of course! Same thing!"

Jazmine looked him in the eyes. "And you believed him?"

He stopped mid chew. "What you mean?"

"You said the last time you saw your nephew he was on his way to meet Toni, right?"

"Yeah."

"So, he gets killed and Toni doesn't? It couldn't have happened out in the open, because if it had, his body would've turned up. At a streetlight, at the club, wherever. No . . . wherever it happened, had to be somewhere he was *going*. He had to have arrived," she reasoned.

Jazmine could tell his wheels were turning. Divide and conquer. It wasn't that she didn't trust Miss Toni, but in the game, it was always better to make sure your allies didn't trust one another so they could never unite against *you*.

"So, you sayin' that faggot muhfucka had somethin' to do with my nephew's death and that *bitch* ass Swag runnin' up on *me?*" he questioned, getting more vexed with every word.

"I'm not saying *anything*; I'm simply telling you, look at every angle. I picked Toni for our arrangement because he *can* be trusted, but I will take a closer look. Until then, you don't say nothin' or move on Toni, are we clear?" Jazmine warned firmly.

Kingfish glared.

"Are we clear?" she repeated.

He pointed at her. "If that faggot—"

"If that faggot had something to do with it, he's playing *me*, and *nobody* does that. I'll take care of it," she assured him.

When he lowered the temperature on his gaze and returned to eating, she knew she had gotten her point across.

"Now . . . back to Swag. I can get him," she remarked.

"Then what are you waiting for?"

"It won't be easy. I'm going to need at least ten of your best men."

"I'll give you twenty!"

"Even better." She smiled, though he knew not why.

"When you need 'em?"

"The sooner the better."

"I'll be in touch ASAP."

Jazmine stood. She looked at the hot sauce drenched gizzards. There was so much, it looked like soup.

"You know one of the leading causes of death amongst black men is high blood pressure."

"And you know pneumonia is the leading cause of death amongst black women from all them cold and lonely nights . . . and runnin' your goddamn mouth is the reason!" he spat back with a chuckle.

When she pulled off, she didn't know she was like Tupac. All eyes on her . . . Matson's to be exact.

-11-

Since he had her car tagged with the GPS chip, he didn't have to tail her, and risk being spotted. He simply allowed her to reach her destination, then followed the beep. As soon as he saw that she was at Kingfish, he knew she was at the top of the food chain. Kingfish was the biggest dealer in the city, but no one could get anything on him. Now, he felt he would. On both of them. It was time to get a warrant to bug their communications.

Satisfied with the discovery, he decided to head home. As soon as he was pulling into the driveway, he saw his wife and two little girls in the backyard. They were pruning the flower garden. Sonia looked up and smiled at him. The last thought he remembered was how beautiful she looked, silhouetted in the afternoon sun.

And then his phone rang.

"Yeah."

"Yeah yourself, sexy," Rain purred.

Staring at his wife with such a pussy cat purring in his ear, he felt like he'd been caught cheating.

"I–uh–uh– I can't," he stammered, then took a deep breath.

The man in him knew what he needed to do. Let it go. He didn't need Rain anymore. He felt he had enough to get a warrant. He could simply say, "I can't do this. I love my wife."

He had all but decided to do it.

And then he heard it.

A soft whisper . . .

"I'm not the type of woman to wait for wh–wh–what I want," Rain moaned, "I was thinking about you fucking this pussy."

Matson was stuck. He wanted to be a good man, but God . . . damn . . . her voice sounded soooo soft, and all he could think about was the way that dildo slid in and out, the cream of her cum coating it like warm syrup.

"Shhhhitt," she hissed, "this pussy on fire, daddy. When you gonna cummmm . . ."

His dick was so hard, it hurt.

"Wh-where are you?" he asked, voice hoarse and choked with lust.

"Almost there!" she squealed, then her moan warbled, and he knew she had just cum from the way she breathed.

"I'm . . . I'm on my way."

He hung up. Sonia looked up when he started the car again. She picked up her phone and called him. "Where are you going, baby?"

"I . . . just got a call . . . my investigation . . ."

Matson knew he would regret this for the rest of his life . . .

But it is usually the things we regret the deepest, that we enjoy the most. It was the anticipation of the latter and not the shame of the former that pressed the gas and not the brake. Still inside, the battle raged, as the sunset and moon rose, hiding his tracks in the shadows.

No! We don't need to do this!

We need the shoe size! If we can place her at the scene of Swag's murder, we're in! said his dark side, masking itself as the voice of reason.

You're making a mistake!

You're doing your job!

The dark side had the advantage. It didn't have to convince him, it simply had to buy time until he got to the condo and his other head took over. Which was exactly what happened when Rain answered the door in a tight tank top, chocolate chip nipples pressed against the fabric like a kid's face up to a candy store window and a pair of lace boy shorts which had 'Rip me!' written all over it.

"You like what you see?" she purred.

He stepped through the door. She frowned slightly.

"How did you know where I live?"

The words exploded in his brains. He had slipped, and there was only one response. He smothered the question with a kiss like a pillow over the face of a sleeping witness.

She devoured the kiss because lust is the enemy of thought; it simply feels. His dick grew hard against her. Hard like human steel. She gripped him through his pants, and he let out a deep throated grunt.

Finally tasting the lips he had fantasized about had him feeling drunk and savage. He squeezed her fat juicy ass until she groaned like he had put his dick in it. His fingers caught in the lace. He didn't hesitate to do what it was asking for.

Riiiiippppp!

It was like ripping the wrappers off passion fruit as her fragrance floated to his nose. Rain wrapped her legs around his waist, and he staggered like a drunken sailor on stormy seas up the hall, knocking a picture from the wall on his way.

When he got her to the room, clothes flew everywhere, each moment, a moment too long to wait to slide inside her. Rain grabbed herself behind the knees, pulling them to her chest. Her clean-shaven pussy sat out plump and dripping.

"Ooh babbby, put it in!" she begged.

He fumbled with the condom. He put it on too tight. He exploded inside of her. *It* exploded inside of her, gathering uselessly at the base of his dick. But he had gone too far to turn back. The feel of her tight, wet pussy around his dick and her hot, hungry moans in his ear was enough to make him risk being raw.

Besides . . . it felt like heaven.

###########

As soon as Jazmine pulled up and saw Matson's car, her whole body tensed.

"What the hell?" she mumbled.

Why was he there? Her diabolical mind shot through a string of scenarios, except the right one because there was no context for coincidence to her way of thinking.

She checked herself in the mirror, took a deep breath and got out. She pictured walking in and finding him there ready to pounce.

She didn't know he already had.

Until she opened the door.

"Oh, Tony! To–Tony, oh my god, Tony!" Rain screamed.

Tony?

Nooooo, the thought stretched from worry to wonder.

Jazmine quietly tiptoed to the open bedroom door. All she saw was Rain spread eagle, toes damn near touching the headboard and Matson in push up position trying to drive her through the mattress.

Jazmine's eyes exploded, and she had to cover her mouth so she wouldn't blurt out, *"What?"* She leaned against the wall, out of sight, letting it sink in.

"What you think about a threesome?" Rain had asked.

Rain had said his name was . . . "Tony."

Never in a million years would she have guessed strait-laced Matson, *married*, Matson, by the book Matson would be in *her* bed. Fucking!

"I got this motherfucka now," she whispered to herself with glee.

Jazmine took out her iPhone and set it to record video, then stripped down ass naked except for her stiletto sandals. He had slipped, but she was so intent on catching *him* slipping, that she slipped *herself*. Because she forgot one thing . . .

She held the iPhone up as she entered the bedroom.

"Goddamn, Rain!" he grunted.

"Baby, you standin' up in it, oh fuck!"

Jazmine made sure to set the phone where it would get a constant shot of his face. He didn't even know she was in the bedroom; he was gone. A rack of clowns would've marched through and he would have thought the honking horns were just the squeaking of the bed. He was totally oblivious, until he felt Jazmine's hand on his shoulder and her lips in his ear.

"Mind if I join you?"

His eyes shot to her face. They were glazed, but she could see the hate trying to charge through. The fruity taste of her tongue trapped it in a bubble of lust. He was balls deep in chocolate and had a tongue full of caramel. He felt like he was stuck in a candy jar and had to eat his way out.

Jazmine ran her tongue down his neck and came up behind him, massaging his ass.

"I want to see you beat that pussy from the back," she cooed.

Rain turned over and cocked her full, luscious ass up in the air, face on the pillow, looking back at him, lip bit.

"Make me feel it in my stomach," she sang breathlessly.

And he did with every stroke. Her ass jiggled and bounced, driving him crazy just watching. Jazmine kissed down his back, ran her tongue along the crack of his ass and didn't stop until she was under him, sucking his balls and the base of his dick and Rain's pussy lips at the same time. They both cried out, enjoying the extra sensation like the cherry on top of the most delicious cake.

"Ohhh, Daddy, your tongue!" Rain gasped. "I'm cummm . . ."

The sound of Matson's strokes became smacks as Rain's juices coated his dick and Jazmine's tongue. Jazmine pulled his dick out of Rain's creamy pussy and slid it in her mouth, relaxing her throat and taking his whole length.

"Oh fuck!" he barked, the suction of her mouth feeling almost as good as Rain's creamy center.

What was really driving Matson crazy was the eye contact. The devilish cat- eyed slant never left his as he fucked her mouth. He wanted his dick to make her gag, but the deeper he went and the more she didn't, the better it felt and the more he wanted it. He couldn't take it anymore. He snatched his dick out and came all over her face.

"Aaargggh!" he roared, never having cum so hard and long.

The spasm made him hunchback, but the sight of Jazmine with his cum all over her face, made him instantly hard again.

"Bend over," he growled.

She smirked seductively, then flipped over. Rain kissed and licked her face. Matson pushed up in her pussy.

"No, put it in my ass," Jazmine cooed, wanting him to feel as savage as possible.

He didn't hesitate. He rammed his rod deep in her tight hole. She squealed with pain and delight.

"Yes, fuck my ass, fuck my ass! I know you wanted to, hated to want to, but you in it now. Tell me how it feels," Jazmine moaned.

Matson felt it so good, he could hardly speak. The hate he had for her; he was expressing through lust. It was more than grudge fucking, it was contempt.

And he never felt better.

He didn't last long, and when he came, once the spasm passed and she had collapsed on top of Rain in a fit of giggles, that's when he saw it.

On her upper right shoulder blade . . .

The brand . . .

The double dragon.

His head may've been fucked up by the mind-blowing sex he had and the scrumptious vision of Rain and Jazmine's heavenly bodies, but he knew he had his answer from earlier.

I got this bitch now, he thought deliciously to himself, not knowing he was already got.

Jazmine used her foot to caress his stomach then up to his chest and said, "See. I knew we could get along."

He caught her foot right before she put it to his mouth and his mind screamed, "Five!"

Matson held her tiny, little sexy foot, kissed the big toe and smiled. "I guess you were right."

Both looked at the other, thinking, *If you only knew...*

"Well, I don't know about y'all, but I need a drink," Jazmine snickered, getting up. "Can I—never mind, I'll just bring the bottle."

Jazmine walked out and Matson began to get dressed. Rain got on her knees behind him and hugged his neck.

"Don't tell me, you have to go so soon. When will I see you again?"

He sighed then looked at her. "Rain . . . I had fun. But I do love my wife . . . I don't think you will," he replied.

Rain smiled graciously.

"I understand. I guess you just had an itch, huh? I'm glad I was the one to scratch it."

He shared a laugh that felt like a parting handshake.

Matson dressed. When he bent to tie his shoe, he saw Jazmine's stiletto and knew what he would find. He rolled it upright. The big (5) on the sole only confirmed what he already knew.

Hers was the footprint in blood.

He started to walk out.

"If you get that itch," Rain said, then put her hand to her ear, "Call me."

Matson winked and walked out.

In the kitchen he saw Jazmine and he walked in. He couldn't help but admire her perfect body. The way she moved like a cat. Fluid. He felt his lower self stir, but he was back in control.

"I got hungry while I was in here," Jazmine said, her back to him as she fixed a sandwich. She looked over her shoulder at him invitingly. "You want some?"

He knew she wasn't talking about food. Neither was he.

"Yeah . . . actually, I do." Matson walked up behind her. He wanted to feel her reaction.

"Some answers, starting with . . . this," he said, tracing the brand with his fingers.

Jazmine's voice caught in her throat . . . that's what she forgot.

The way her body stiffened, her shaky reply of, ". . . a tattoo," came out unconvincingly.

He chuckled.

"What a coincidence. That dead girl, you know, the one from earlier? She had the same one. Remember?"

He was toying with her. She hated to be toyed with, but she had slipped, so she knew all she could do was try and run damage control.

"It's a popular tattoo. Sort of like a panther or a rose."

"I'm sure . . . who's Swag?"

It was like he was hitting her with body blow after body blow.

Jazmine winced.

Did he know? Her mind whirled in a panic.

"Who?" she replied, the word sounding like a crack.

"He was murdered, a few years back. It's a cold case, very little evidence, except for a woman's footprint in the blood. Size five . . . I think I may have a lead. Whaddaya say we re-open the case?" Matson taunted her, then unable to resist, slapped her ass and added, "*Partner.*"

Jazmine jumped on contact because her nerves were on edge. Matson left chuckling. She stood at the counter, hot and cold. Cold, because he could positively link her to the scene of Swag's murder, and as a police officer, not having made this known could cost her, her whole career and the plan she had in motion.

Her first thought was . . . kill him. But who had he already told? Who else knew? She had to get that footprint, but she didn't dare move until she knew exactly the situation.

Then she remembered that things were not that bad. She had him, too . . . iPhone. What would he do to protect his marriage?

Jazmine smiled to herself because she loved a challenge. It brought out the best in her. She grabbed her roast beef and mustard sandwich along with the bottle of Zinfandel. When she got to the bedroom, she broke Rain off half the sandwich and the bottle of Zinfandel.

"Do you know who that was?" Jazmine asked, smirking.

"No, why? You know him?" Rain responded, face full of sandwich.

Jazmine nodded.

"He's a cop . . . actually, my partner."

Rain's eyes got big, but her quick street mind caught on.

"*That's* why he knew where I lived and how he *accidentally* bumped into me at the salon! That muhfucka been watchin' us, huh?"

Jazmine nodded her head and they fell silent for a moment.

"Where is Malaya?" Jazmine asked; her main focus was Matson and what he had planned, but in the back of her mind she thought about Malaya and how she hadn't disturbed them.

"My mom came to get her for a few hours," Rain answered; her thoughts still on Tony and the fact that he had played her.

"Baby, I'm sorry. I didn't—"

Knowing where she was going with her statement, Jazmine held her hand up to silence her and smiled.

"You couldn't have known. He played it slick . . . but I played it slicker. Wanna watch a movie?" Her smile turned into a devilish grin.

She grabbed her iPhone and showed Rain their sex tape. Rain burst out laughing.

"Daddy, you are too cold! I guess he will be seeing me again after all!"

Jazmine swigged from the bottle. She knew she had Matson by one nut, but she needed to have them both, and she knew just how to do it.

But first . . .

Matson couldn't go straight home. He just couldn't. He had never cheated on his wife, so he didn't know what to do. The way he felt; he knew she'd see it all over him.

He decided to have a drink . . . or two . . . or three. He didn't really have a plan besides waiting until he thought she'd be asleep, then sneak in like a stranger, shower, and get in the bed. He wouldn't even get a chance to kiss his daughters before they went to sleep like he did every night.

Stolen moments steal other moments, precious moments, moments that leave Grand Canyon sized holes in your conscience. He glanced at himself in the mirror over the bar. He felt dirty. He had set out to prove Jazmine was dirty, only to prove he was, too.

"Every single one of us . . . is the devil inside," he mumbled into his rum and coke.

His phone chimed. Something told him who it was. He looked. It was a video message. As soon as he saw it loading, his conscience screamed, "I told you!"

He almost didn't have to look, but he did anyway.

"Goddamn, Rain!" he heard himself say in the tape.

Seeing himself in action almost made him want to throw up. He stopped the video. His phone rang a few minutes later.

"I guess you're calling to gloat," he said as soon as he picked up, numb from his emotions and the alcohol.

"I have no idea what you're talking about. I just called to say . . . maybe we *shouldn't* re-open that cold case. Let's leave all the bones in the closet," Jazmine proposed.

Matson snorted. Downed his drink. "Coleman . . . it ever bother you that you have no soul?"

Jazmine laughed. "Welcome to the club."

Click.

-12-

The mayor stood at his office window and looked out over the spread of the city. His chest swelled as he thought, *I run this city.*

He was the head nigguh in charge; in a city full of heady nigguhs, they all bowed to him. He got a piece of everything that moved through the city. He had the city council wrapped around his finger, and all city construction was being done through companies he controlled.

"Next stop, the Governor's mansion." He chuckled to himself. His thoughts were interrupted when his secretary knocked on the door.

"Yeah."

She entered. Even behind the wire rimmed glasses, it was obvious why she had the job. She looked like Nia Long, bowlegs and all.

"Mr. Mayor, Detective Coleman to see you."

James Joyner looked at his watch with a slight frown.

"It's barely eleven. I thought she said two?"

"I like to be early," Jazmine replied, stepping through the door, then turned to the secretary, adding, "Run along now."

The secretary looked like, *No this bitch didn't.*

Joyner cleared his throat.

"Denise, I've got it from here."

The secretary left. Jazmine made her way to the large window behind his desk and enjoyed the view.

"I bet you were just standing here thinking I'm the man, huh?" she snickered.

"I'm just a humble servant of the people," he replied.

"Nice sound bite. Now . . . take off your clothes."

"What!" he squawked.

Jazmine sighed.

"James, James, James . . . you know the drill. You don't trust me, and I don't trust you. I tell you two and come at eleven, and when we talk you get naked. Simple."

"I'm not wearing a wire."

"Then you have nothing to hide." She smirked. "Except maybe shame?"

He stripped down to his boxers, socks, and shoes.

"See."

"Lots. Bathroom," she ordered.

They stepped into his personal bathroom which sported a marble counter and large mirror. Jazmine sat on the counter.

"I want to know if I'm under investigation."

"Not–not that I know of," Joyner stammered, taken aback by the force of her question.

She hopped off the counter. "What do you mean, you don't know? We've got a fuckin' arrangement! You're supposed to cover my ass with the city!"

"I am! Evidently, it doesn't need covering if I haven't heard anything!" he reasoned.

She glared at him. "Don't fuckin' play with me, James! I'm workin' something very big here, and it's gonna make us *very* rich."

"Believe me, I'm playing my part," he assured her.

"You better be," she warned.

She held his gaze a moment longer, then her eyes fell to his crotch. His dick wasn't hard, but it had stiffened enough so the head peeked out.

"Looks like somebody wants to say hello." She giggled.

He stuffed it back in, but it fell out again. He couldn't lie. Just being close to Jazmine's sexy ass was enough to get the average man's blood pumping.

"I noticed your secretary wasn't wearing any panties. Did you tell her not to?"

He cleared his throat.

"I–I don't know anything about that."

His dick got a little harder.

"I'm not wearing any panties either . . . and my pussy's sweeter. You want a taste?" Jazmine cooed in his ear.

"Coleman, I'm a married man," he replied, but his dick got even harder. His dick was like Pinocchio's nose. Every time he lied, it got longer.

Jazmine moaned so sensually in his ear, he sprung to full length.

"Touch it for me. I want to see you cum. I want to see that snake spit," she cooed, taking his hand and wrapping it around his shaft.

She kept her hand on his, pumping, until he got the rhythm himself.

"Are you going to fuck her when I leave? Imagine it's me you're fuckin . . . I'm bent over your desk looking back at you. Ohhhh, daddy, put it in my ass . . . I love it in my ass; it makes my pussy squirt."

"Oh Jesus!" He trembled, looking at her through the mirror, pumping faster.

"Your big fat dick all in my tight little ass, and I'm squirming all over your desk. Daddy, oh god! Daddy, it–

it hurts, daddy . . . Oh fuck! Hurt me, daddy, ohhhhh," she moaned, and it sounded like she was melting into a pure orgasm.

Cum shot out and sprayed the mirror like splashes of white paint. Joyner bent over the sink, breathing hard. Jazmine got in his ear and said, "Now, what have we learned? We've learned that if you even *think* of fucking me . . . you'll be fuckin' *yourself.*"

With that, she walked out.

-13-

"Ay yo, why are we meetin' these nigguhs at a fuckin' faggot club?" one thug asked another, as they drove to the rendezvous point.

The other thug shrugged. "Kingfish said that's the spot. What the fuck it matter?" the first thug griped. "Man, pull around back. I 'on't want nobody seein' me go up in there."

He was doing exactly what Jazmine wanted them to do. She knew Kingfish's gunners would feel uncomfortable meeting at the Pink Diamond, so they'd enter through the most discreet means. For those who didn't, Milly was out front to let them know, "Go, mon. Park in the back."

There were twenty-two in all, and they were all carrying big guns. AR .15s and AKs, Choppers, and fully automatic machine guns with necklaces of .50 caliber bullets around their necks like Somali pirates. Miss Toni took one look, shook his head, and mumbled to himself, "This shit better work, or we some dead motherfuckers."

Jazmine leaned on the bar nursing a drink, with flawless make-up and looking very much like the baddest bitch in the club. The Christian Dior mini skirt with the red bottom stilletos commanded that heads turn. Kingfish's top lieutenant, Blaze, saw her and made his way over.

"You must be who I'm looking for," he salivated, looking her up and down.

"What makes you say that?"

"Wishful thinking." He smiled.

Jazmine laughed and held out her hand. "I'm Jazmine."

He took her hand and kissed it. "I'm Blaze. Nice to meet you."

She looked him up and down. He was definitely a cutie, looking like a thuggish Drake. Too bad there wasn't more time.

"What are you drinking?" she asked.

"Shit, ma, whatever you put in my glass. Bathwater, perhaps?"

Jazmine laughed.

"That was cute. Bartenders! Drinks on me and keep em' comin," she instructed.

The waitresses made sure that every gunner had a drink . . . or two . . . or three. The night wore on and some of the gunners got impatient.

"Ay yo, I thought we was supposed to be movin' on that nigguh Swag."

"Yeah, yo. I'm ready to get the fuck outta here!"

Comments like those reached Miss Toni's ear as he sashayed through the crowd. He stopped when he saw three gunners standing at the opposite end of the bar. The shortest one caught his eye, looking like Morris Chestnut.

"Hmph, what's *your* name?" Miss Toni asked in his huskiest voice. Morris looked him up and down and spat, "Man, get your faggot ass out my face!"

"Wait a minute, little nigguh, 'cause mother does have her mannish ways," he huffed, fists balled just in case the little nigguh wanted to start something.

"Man!" Morris barked, blinked, blinked, wobbled and staggered.

"I think you better sit." Miss Toni smirked as Morris fell flat on his face, and he added, "Down."

But it wasn't only him. All over the club, one by one the woozy spread like cancer.

"I'm saying, Jazmine, I'm trying to soup like purssss," Blaze said, but his words slurred and they made no sense.

"Huh?" she asked, as if she didn't know what was happening.

Blaze wobbled.

"Whoa, whooooa. Shit, I'm niiiice." He smiled, right before trying to sit on the stool.

He missed and fell flat on his ass, sleep.

One thug, right before he passed out, looked around at all his people falling out and slurred, "Izzzzz a set uuuup!"

He pulled his gun from his waist right before falling on the couch. Jazmine sipped her drink with a smile as she looked around. The only people standing were the twins, Miss Toni, and the bartender. All of Kingfish's men were snoring from the powerful sleeping pills that spiked every drink they had.

"Get the zip ties," Jazmine told Milly.

Within fifteen minutes they had every gunners' hands bound behind their back with the plastic zip ties police use in mass arrest situations.

"Goddamn, it took long enough. I was starting to get nervous," Miss Toni remarked, limp-wristed hand over his heart.

Jazmine started for the door.

"You know what to do with them," she remarked, because it had already been discussed. The hole had already been dug, and the concrete was waiting to be poured. She was burying these nigguhs alive.

"Ah Jaz . . . let me speak with you, thug," Miss Toni requested.

Jazmine walked over.

"Now you know mother has done *all* you've asked, and bitch you *know* I would walk through hell in gasoline stilettos for you, but look at this," he said, then squatted down next to Morris and rolled him over on his back. She grabbed his dick through his jeans. The print was massive. "Now, look at that! That is simply too much to go to waste. Let mother keep this one in my dirty lil' cage for a few days, hmmmm?"

Jazmine chuckled and shook her head.

"Two days, Toni."

Miss Toni kissed her cheek. "That's *all* mother needs!"

-14-

The downtown arena was packed. Teenage girls from a hundred-mile radius had come to see the OMG Girlz. Traffic in and around the arena crawled like snails slithering through mud.

"Never again," were the words Sonia would repeat over and over throughout the night, until she'd look at the smile on Bianca's face and her heart would melt.

The crowd was monstrous, a headache just waiting to happen, especially when Sonia had seen what Bianca's best friend, Tammy, was wearing. She hadn't noticed in the car, because she was in a hurry. It was dark and she really didn't care, until she saw that apparently Tammy's mother didn't either. Tammy was wearing a too-tight midriff that hugged her budding breasts and exposed her belly ring, thankfully a clip-on. Her capris were so tight Sonia could see her thong print.

Her thong print! She was twelve years old!

Sonia fully intended on saying something to Tammy's mother. But it wasn't just Tammy. The *majority* of the young girls at the show were dressed like little hoochies, walking with mothers who proved the apple didn't fall far from the tree.

"Mommy, can I get a T-shirt?" Bianca beamed.

Sonia took one look at the line and replied, "Later," hoping she'd forget.

The show was loud, the music basically noise, and the singing, a melodious shriek, but that was what was passing as music to the teenaged and preteen audience.

Bianca was in heaven . . . until she looked into the face of hell. She had first seen him shortly after entering the arena. The strange-looking pale man. He looked as if he had no color. Like a black and white aberration in a world full of color. When she looked, he smiled at her and tipped his brim. She smiled politely. He moved on. When she saw him again, his whole aura had transformed. The bluish tinged stage lights seemed to make him glow in the dark, like one of those glow sticks kept in the freezer to keep it functioning. It was an eerie glow, and his black marble eyes seemed to bore through her. He didn't smile this time . . .

He blew a kiss.

Fear leapt into Bianca's breasts, and her breath caught in her throat.

"Mommy, look," Bianca tapped Sonia.

"Huh?" Sonia squinted to hear her over the blare.

"Look!" Bianca pointed.

He was gone. All Sonia saw were delirious, screaming girls.

"What is it, baby?"

"Nothing." Bianca scanned the crowd a couple of times, then breathed a sigh of relief . . . he was gone.

After the show, the first thing Bianca said was, "Mommy, can we get the T-shirt now?"

Sonia chuckled. "Yes baby, we can get it now."

"Mrs. Matson, I have to go to the bathroom," Tammy chimed in, although she only wanted to *go* to the bathroom.

The dark-skinned cutie with the gold toothed grin was standing over there.

"Y'all go to the bathroom, I'll get in line," Sonia instructed them, and it would be the one sentence that would haunt her nightmares, echoing over and over and...

##########

Tammy grabbed Bianca's hand and headed toward the bathroom.

"Ohh, Bianca, look! No–don't look–look like, kinda look. You see him? He is so foine!" she remarked excitedly.

It was hard for Bianca to look and not to look at the same time, so she didn't see him until he stepped up and said to Tammy, "Damn, lil' mama, what's your name?"

Tammy started twirling her shoulders like the little girl she really was.

"Tammy."

"Tammy, let's *go!*" Bianca huffed, because the situation didn't feel right.

"I–I have to go!" Tammy repeated, batting her lashes.

"Look! The stage door! It's OMG!" somebody yelled.

Yelling O-M-G in a room full of little girls is like yelling "Fire!" in a crowded theatre. Except instead of running from, they ran *to*. It was like a dam bursting, as a wave of screaming teens washed across the arena.

Sonia got swept up in the wave, standing in line. The crowd of never ending teen girls went by, and she scanned them looking for Bianca. But when she didn't see her, she glanced at the bathroom line.

No Bianca.

The bathroom line was too long for Bianca to have made it in already. She decided to walk over. Her eyes scanned the line.

"Bianca!" she called out, even though the crowd was still noisy.

No Bianca.

She got a little more anxious.

"Bianca!"

Without hesitation, she skipped the line and went in the bathroom.

"Hey!" the lady next in line, protested.

"I'm looking for my daughter," Sonia tossed over her shoulder, then looked around and called out, "Bianca, are you in here?"

No . . . Bianca.

Her motherly instinct shrieked in her ear. Her heart rate sped up triple time.

"Bianca!" she screamed, bursting out of the bathroom.

The room spun around her as she looked around and around and...

The somebody who hollered about OMG was one of Satan's thugs.

They needed a cover. They were all in place. When the crowd rose in one voice and one body, the thugs cuffed Bianca and Tammy's mouths and noses with a chemically soaked handkerchief. Their muffled cries didn't even register in the cacophony of screams. The chemicals were powerful and almost instantaneous.

Their little bodies went limp, and thugs carried them off, heads on their shoulders as if they were asleep. Four more little girls would be snatched up that night the same way.

That's when Sonia knew.

"Keisha! Keisha, where are you?"

"Oh my God, Tonia!"

"I can't find my daughter!"

The anguish was palpable. All laughter stopped and was replaced with sobs, until Sonia bubbled up and blew forth so loud, so clear, so deep that her voice seemed to fill the arena, echo in the parking lot, and awaken the city . . .

"Biiiannnncaaaaaa!"

-15-

They were packed as tight as frozen fish filets. That's what they were packaged to looked like. The crates were sealed tight as they were lowered from the ship and loaded onto the truck. Several of Kingfish's goons stood around, armed and eyes peeled.

Big D, the lieutenant in charge, checked his watch.

"Where the fuck is Blaze?" he mumbled to himself.

There was just entirely too much coke for seven thugs to hold down. Usually, on major pickups like these, there'd be at least thirty.

"You ready?" Swag spat into the walkie talkie, squatting behind a large metal shipping container.

"Yep, yep," Miss Toni replied over the air.

It was time for some action.

Bbbbbbrrrppppp!

Miss Toni's machine ripped like it was tearing a hole through the night itself, opening a murderous wound. The first two thugs fired, spun, and dropped before the other five had a chance to fire back.

"Shit!" Big D swore, diving for cover. "Go! Go!" he yelled at the truck driver.

The truck driver rumbled to life, but before he could switch a gear, Lilly took aim from atop of a shipping container, put the driver's head in the crosshairs of the scope, and just like in a video game, blew his brains all over the passenger seat, causing a fine spray of brain matter to sprinkle the windshield.

The other five thugs did their best, but they were outnumbered and outgunned. Miss Toni's team may've been filled with males who weren't men and females that weren't women, but they were all definitely killers.

Big D made a dash for the truck's cabin. He had to get the coke. He let off several rounds of his automatic, leapt up onto the truck's running board and snatched open the door, only to stare the barrel of Swag's .45 straight down the pipe.

"Goin' somewhere?" Swag smirked.

"Y–y–you got it, you, you got it," Big D stammered, letting the gun fall from his hand as he raised his arms.

"Step down . . . easy," Swag warned.

Big D did exactly that, right into the waiting arms of Miss Toni. He jacked him up by the collar and slammed him face first into the side of the truck. Swag climbed through the cabin and stood behind Big D, gun to his ear.

"Today's your lucky day. I'm gonna let you live. Thank me," Swag said. Big D gritted his teeth. Swag pushed the pistol into his head.

"Thank me."

"Thank you," Big D grumbled.

"You tell Kingfish forget being partners. I want it all. Tell him Swag said it. Got me?"

"You know you a fuckin' dead man, right? You fuckin' wit' pros and don't even know it!" Big D taunted.

Swag chuckled. "So are you."

With that, she hit him hard at the base of his skull, knocking him out cold. As soon as his body hit the ground, one of Miss Toni's team members jumped behind the wheel of the rig, then Swag and the rest melted back into the shadows from whence they came.

#########

Kingfish didn't only have a big appetite in the kitchen, he had one in the bedroom too. "Goddamn, daddy, oohh you fuckin' this pussy good!" the girl riding his dick squealed. "Ki–Ki–King, oohh looooove!" the girl sitting on his face sang. "Ffffffff!" the third girl curled up beside him was sniffing coke. All three were barely legal because he liked his bitches young and dumb.

He fed them a constant stream of dick and drugs, not necessarily in that order. A fourth girl, just as naked as the other three, walked in on Gucci heels, holding a cordless phone.

"Kingfish," she called out, holding the phone with a limp wrist.

"Hmmmm," he mumbled, with a face full of ass.

"Telephone."

Annoyed, he pushed the girl to lift up. "Bitch, I'm busy!"

"I think you're gonna want to take this."

"Why?"

"It's Big D . . . and he cryin'."

When thugs cry . . .

##########

This could not be happening.

No way could this be happening . . .

But it was. The tears on his cheeks were real. The wracking sobs of his wife were real on his shoulder. The flashing lights of the police cars, the squawk of walkie talkies and the murmur of the crowd told Matson it was real. This was really a crime scene, and his daughter had been abducted.

How could this happen? he thought, bewildered.

"Baby . . . I *promise*, we're going to get her back," Matson vowed, holding his wife tight, with everything in him.

Was this his punishment for a moment of indiscretion?

The question popped in his mind but was quickly followed by a prayer . . . *Lord, please forgive me and bring my baby home safe . . .*

Over his shoulder, he saw Jazmine pull up and start toward them. His body stiffened. His wife looked up at him.

"Baby . . . what's wrong?"

"Nothing," he lied as Jazmine approached.

Their eyes met. His were hard and unyielding. Hers said truce.

"Detective, I came as soon as I heard. You must be Mrs. Matson. I'm Jazmine Coleman, Tony's partner. I'm so sorry, but we will get her back," Jazmine remarked, then gave Sonia a warm hug.

She wasn't lying when she said she came as soon as she heard. Fresh off the Kingfish robbery, her Swag goatee and green contacts were in the book bag under the passenger seat.

But her eyes were lying. With Jazmine, there was never a truce. She used every situation to her benefit. The abduction of a child was no different.

Her and Matson's eyes met again over his wife's shoulder. This time, his gaze was skeptically softer. Her words had hit the mark.

"Th–thank you, Detective Coleman." Sonia sniffed.

"Jazmine," Jazmine corrected her.

Sonia mustered a smile. "Jazmine. I'm Sonia."

"Now, I'm sure Tony's already been over this with you, but I'd like to be brought up to speed directly," she requested, pulling out a pen and pad. "So please, start from the beginning."

Sonia took a deep breath and told her everything. Jazmine took notes, asking all the right questions. Matson was strangely comforted by her professionalism. Besides, he was too close to the situation, so having another detective back him up was a plus.

As she finished, Jazmine looked at Sonia, took a deep breath, and said, "Now this is *strictly* routine, but I need to ask. Is there anyone that would want to hurt you or your daughter?"

Sonia shook her head, glanced at Matson, then answered, "No, no, nobody."

Jazmine looked at Matson.

"Detective."

"Not at all."

Jazmine nodded. "I think that's about it. Tony, why don't you take Sonia home? I'll wrap things up for you here."

Matson took one look at his wife and saw how exhausted she looked.

"Thanks . . . Detective," Matson replied, reluctantly.

Jazmine smiled. "Not a problem."

Jazmine watched Matson and Sonia walking off. Her conniving mind going a million miles an hour, but deep down, something totally different was beginning to bubble . . .

-16-

They were little more than modified dog kennels. Cages; packed with naked human flesh. The floor was cold concrete, made even colder by the fact that they were deep underground in the basement of a large warehouse. The cages were from floor to ceiling, about the size of a living room and lined side by side, from wall to wall. Each cage had many naked females, made sisters of circumstance. The fear was so thick it became a stench. A heavy fog, like the heat of humans herded had combined with the moisture of the tears to create a humidity that clung to the air.

"Wh-wh-what are we going to do?" Tammy sobbed uncontrollably. Bianca held her tight, even though she was probably more scared than Tammy.

"God will protect us," Bianca whispered, rocking her and humming a song Sonia would hum to her if she were there.

Bianca looked at all the naked bodies. It made them all seem so . . . dehumanized. Her eyes fell on a female two cages across. She lay on her back, unmoving. Corpse like. The girl was so skinny her ribs protruded grotesquely. Once, she had been thick and curvaceous, but since she had been snatched from the motel and raped repeatedly, her sister killed by a car, and her white friend strangled right there in the cage, her spirit was broken. She had stopped eating and had begun to waste away.

Bianca only knew she felt even sadder looking at the girl. A few minutes later, two goons entered, walking between the cages like thug COs, keys jingling. They went to the girl's cage and opened it. One stepped in and stood over the girl. He kicked her thigh to see if she was even breathing.

"Still ain't gonna eat, bitch?"

She didn't say a word.

"Then I'ma give you what you want."

He grabbed her by her bony ankles and dragged her out the cage, like someone would drag a sack of potatoes. Bianca was so intent on looking at the girl being dragged, so intent on the total composure of her face, that she didn't even hear the other goon open the cage she was in. She didn't, until she felt Tammy being ripped from her arms.

"Bianca!" Tammy screamed.

"Tammy!" Bianca screamed.

The thug from the arena snatched her up and over his shoulder.

"Come on, lil' mama, we got some unfinished business!"

"Noooooo!" Tammy groaned.

The thug laughed as he carried her off.

"Get off my friend! Let her go!" Bianca yelled, banging and shaking the cage's fence.

A few moments later, a single gunshot echoed through every cage. They knew the starving girl was finally free. But it made everyone think that death was the only way out. Tammy's screams echoed out.

"Get off her!" Bianca screamed, crying hysterically.

"Baby . . . please. Shhhhh."

Bianca looked up and saw the face of an angel. But she wasn't an angel. She was one of them, but looking through the fence at Bianca, the angel saw herself a long time ago . . .

The angel's name was Alicia.

Her mother, who had never set foot in a church before, had taken her to a large church on the outskirts of New Orleans when she was twelve years old. When the pastor said, "Come on down this morning!" her mother turned to her and said, "Come on."

Alicia didn't understand what it meant to be saved. She didn't even know she was lost. But she was, the moment her mother met her new boyfriend, the boyfriend who said he loved her sooo much, but that a child . . . complicated things. Her mother, who had had Alicia at fourteen, never having been a child, didn't know how to love one. But she knew what it meant to love a man.

It meant her daughter needed to be . . . saved.

The albino pastor scared her. He was as white as a ghost with eyes like empty sockets. His hand felt cold and clammy when he shook her little hand in a room in the back of the church.

"Alicia, it's very nice to meet you." He smiled, but it looked more like a leer.

"Pastor, I'm–I'm so glad you can take in my little girl. Things have been so hard lately," her mother stuttered, tears brimming.

"Shhh, my child. Everything will be fine. Alicia will be a precious addition to the ministry," he assured her.

Her mother nodded. "Thank the Lord."

When she tried to leave, Alicia clung to her. "Mommy, please don't leave me! I'll be good, I promise!" she sobbed.

But her mother's heart had already turned away, even before she did. The pastor pulled them apart. Alicia cried her little eyes out until her mother disappeared for good.

"Don't cry, child. Don't you love your mommy?" Satan asked tenderly, wiping her tears.

She nodded profusely.

"Don't you trust your mommy?"

"Y-yes."

"Then you know she wouldn't leave you with me if I were bad, right?"

As much as it hurt, Alicia felt he had to be right, and if she were good for her mommy, then she'd come back.

"I-I guess."

He smiled.

"Come."

He held out his hand and she took it. He took her to his large plantation styled house, straight to Aria's room, where Aria waited.

"This is Alicia. Alicia, this is Aria. Aria, welcome her."

Aria reached out and pulled Alicia in for a big hug that Alicia gobbled up.

"Welcome, Alicia."

Satan sat down in the antique rocking chair in the corner of Aria's room, the one he always used on such occasions and crossed his legs.

"Now . . . Alicia. Look at me."

She did.

"Do you love your mommy?"

She nodded again as she did before.

"Yes."

"Then you must trust me, do you understand?"

"Yes, pastor."

He smiled. "Good girl. Now, in order to be a good girl, you must be . . . cleansed. You must be cleansed of all the bad things. You must never lie to me," he explained.

"I won't," Alicia assured him.

"Or disobey me."

"Yes, pastor."

"Now . . . take off your clothes," he told her.

Alicia froze.

"Are you disobeying me, Alicia?"

"No, I-I-I don't want to," she replied, the tears coming back.

"I thought you wanted to be a good girl? Do you think your mommy will really come back to a bad girl?"

His words hit a nerve and made her think he could read minds, but he couldn't, he just knew the mind of a child.

"I want my mommy," she whined softly.

"Then be a good girl," he replied, expression stern.

Slowly, with shaking hands she removed her dress with the flowers and frilly border. When she stood before him in her budding nudeness, he caressed her with his eyes.

"Aria . . . cleanse her."

Aria nodded obediently, then took Alicia's hand and led her over to her four-post bed. She had done this so much; she was numb to Alicia's childish sobs. Satan watched as Aria devoured Alicia's young body, a body that had never known lust, but would soon crave it. When she was done and the room smelled of virginity lost, Satan stood, smiled and said, "See to it that she eats." Then he walked out.

Aria lay on the bed listening to Alicia cry herself to sleep and stared at the ceiling wondering if it's really worth all this to be a good girl . . .

#########

The limo pulled up to the row of boutiques on Canal Place. It was Aria's seventeenth birthday and Satan was treating her to a shopping spree to celebrate. Aria stepped out flanked by two of Satan's thugs, then Satan stepped out looking like Mr. GQ himself.

"Daddy, I know you don't like when I shop, so if you want, you can come back and pick me up," Aria suggested.

"You'd like that, wouldn't you?" he replied, a slight growl in his throat.

She knew what he was getting at.

Swag.

She hadn't seen him since the church, but Satan seemed to be able to sense what she wanted to deny. Deny that she had been thinking about him since his eyes had seemed to rape her the night of the hit, the way she burned his gaze in church, how she murmured his name in French in her sleep.

But that last part she wasn't aware of . . . but Satan was. So, he watched her like a hawk. Because, of all his women, she was the one he wanted to make love him. Because for some reason, she submitted with her body but never with her mind. And he had a problem with that.

"Fine," she replied and went in the store.

Store after store, he stayed with her, until he tired of her perusing.

"Aria, this is the last store," he told her firmly.

She knew not to challenge him. She turned to the saleswoman.

"I would like to try this on."

"Certainly. The dressing rooms are right down this hall." She smiled.

"Merci," Aria replied and headed down the hall carrying the dress.

She went inside and placed the dress on the hook behind the door, then began to undress. When she was down to just her pink bra and panty set, the door opened, and Swag stepped inside.

Aria's voice caught in her throat.

She gasped. "You're not—you can't be here."

"So, call him. He will come. One of us will die. Guess which one," he replied, as always in Creole.

"Then you don't know him well."

"I never said it would be him."

It was right then that she realized what made him such a cold-blooded killer. Because he was prepared to die.

Swag took a step toward her.

"You don't understand," she mumbled, pleading. "Please, you have to go."

The closer he came, the weaker she seemed to get.

He reached out and ran his hand from the hollow of her throat to the flesh of her cleavage. She trembled. His aroma enveloped her. It smelled earthy and pungent but inviting.

"Please . . . "

Swag moved in, pushing his body against hers. He leaned in to kiss her, in one swift motion she pushed him away with one hand and snatched the gun from his waist with the other. She held the gun braced with both hands, aimed at his face.

"You. Have. To. Go," Aria gritted.

Swag could see the watery determination in her eyes, no less firm because of the tears. He knew there was something more holding her back, more than Satan.

He held up his hands. "Okay. I'll go . . . for now."

Slowly but steadily, he reached out and took the gun from her hand, tucked the gun back in place, then repeated, "For now."

He stepped out the door, peeped the hallway, then headed out the back-exit seconds before Satan turned the opposite corner, heading for the dressing room. Only one door was closed. He started to knock, but he stopped and sniffed the air.

He smelled the bayou. A smell like that had no place in a fancy boutique.

Instead of knocking, he barged in.

Aria jumped.

"Oh! You scared me! What's wrong?" she asked.

He looked at her intently, sensing, feeling, knowing, but not wanting to admit something was wrong.

"Nothing," he grumbled.

"How do I look?" She smirked, twirling in the dress.

"Buy it and let's go."

##########

Three weeks later, Love came to New Orleans to expand his reach. He didn't fear running up against Satan because he thought they had a deal.

Three days after Love's arrival, Swag watched his every move at the request of Satan. "I have a problem," Satan had told Swag. "Solve it."

Love and his two shooters went from the Hilton to Calliope projects and back, seldom changing up their routine. Swag could've hit him anywhere along the route, but this time, Swag had a plan of his own.

"Yo, I'm tellin' you, Love, this N'awlins move is sweet as a muhfucka," one of Love's shooters remarked.

Love laughed. "Yeah, I'm glad Gucci talked me into it."

They pulled up to the hotel, parked and went inside. They saw a drunk dude with dreads stagger to the elevator. People shied away from getting on with him. When the elevator returned to the lobby, it was empty. Love and his people stepped on and ascended.

"But I tell you one thing, these N'awlins bitches damn sure know how to drop-drop-drop it like it's hot!" one shooter joked.

They all laughed. Love glanced up at the changing numbers. Somewhere between the ninth and tenth floor, the whole elevator car shook with the sounds of gunshots.

Boom! Boom! Boom!

The first bullet went through the top of one of the shooter's head at an angle that sent fragments of his brain shooting out of his mouth, as if he were throwing up random thoughts.

What the . . . Love's mind exclaimed. Everything was happening so fast he still didn't know where the shots were coming from. The next two shots blew through the other shooter's temple, blowing brain matter all over the elevator panel before his body slumped to the floor. That's when Love found out where the shots were coming from.

"Put your face to the wall," Swag barked from the escape hatch in the ceiling of the elevator.

Love turned, hands raised and faced the wall.

"Yo, the money I got on me ain't even worth all this, player," Love said, trying to sound calm.

Swag climbed down and stopped the elevator between the twelfth and thirteenth floor.

"Turn around . . . slow."

When he did, he saw a familiar face. The drunken dude from the lobby. Now Love knew why the elevator was empty. He glared into Swag's mis-matched eyes.

"Satan. Him want ya dead," Swag announced in broken English, guns aimed.

"Satan? Word, that's how he comin'?" Love remarked, feeling like he had been played.

"He bring you here on his turf, kill you, and take over yours," Swag explained, wondering why Love didn't see it coming. *"Never make a deal with the devil. But I have deal for you."*

Love grunted. "How I know I can trust you?"

"Because you breathin'," Swag reminded him swiftly.

Love looked at him, studied him.

"What's the deal?"

"Give me your number. Go home. I will come to you," Swag explained.

Love looked down at his two men. "I'm supposed to forget you did that?"

Swag shrugged.

"Better them, than you. Satan pay for hit, but you got away."

Swag, keeping his eyes on Love, bent and took the guns from his dead shooters. Then stood back up.

"Remember, go home. I'll be in touch."

Swag climbed back through the escape hatch, leaving Love to thank his lucky stars he was still alive.

##########

"What do you mean he got away?" Satan questioned.

Swag shrugged.

"He's nobody's fool. I was able to get his men, but not him."

Satan and Swag sat in Satan's limo that night. Satan thought hard on the whole scenario. He knew Swag didn't miss. Something didn't add up, something he hadn't figured out, but definitely wouldn't forget.

"Then I owe you nothing."

"You never do," Swag replied, then opened the door.

"Stay away from her. I won't tell you again. If you don't . . . the old woman won't be able to save you," Satan warned without looking at him.

Swag looked back at Satan and replied, "I don't need her to."

He got out of the car, and in his wake, Satan could smell the earthy, pungent odor of the bayou . . .

-17-

For the first time, Kingfish didn't have an appetite. Furious; he paced the floor of his office, huffing from all his blubber, but he kept going, hoping to pace into some kind of solution.

He now owed the Cartel twenty million dollars, and he didn't have so much as an ounce to pay them with, a fact he knew wouldn't make a bit of difference to them. The tick . . . tick . . . tick of the clock over the desk seemed to be ticking off precious seconds of his life. He couldn't take it anymore. He snatched the clock down and smashed it on the floor just as Jazmine walked in.

"Am I interrupting something?" she asked skeptically.

"Close the goddamn door," he grunted, wiping sweat from his brow.

She did, then she sat down.

"I got hit!"

"Hit?" she echoed, as if she didn't know.

"Hit, goddamn. Hit! Robbed! The shipment got jacked by that fuckin' Swag! The nigguh *you* were supposed to handle!" he ranted; but being unable to walk and talk, he plopped his big ass down into his chair.

"He's smarter than I thought," she replied.

"Either that, or you're dumber than you appear," he shot back.

Jazmine chuckled. "Insults, Kingfish?"

"I want my coke! I don't give a fuck what you have to do! Find it!" he ordered.

"What's in it for me?" She smirked.

"A million dollars," he blurted out, hearing the tick... tick . . . in his head.

Jazmine whistled. "Wow . . . you know, for a million dollars I definitely would've found it . . . if I didn't already know where it was."

His eyes shot to her face, relief coloring his cheeks like too much rouge on a whore. "Where?"

"I got it," she replied calmly.

It took Kingfish a second to wrap his head around the thought, like a chess player trying to figure out why his opponent had yelled checkmate.

"You . . . got it?"

She nodded, eyeing him closely. "Actually, I took it when I found out where it would be from your nephew, who Swag—who works for me—killed. That would be all my doing. Any questions?"

Kingfish trembled so hard, she thought he was having a heart attack; ironically, it would've hurt Jazmine if he died, but he wasn't. His rage propelled him out of the chair, and he lunged at her.

Boc!

She let him get around the desk, before taking out her gun and shooting him in the shoulder.

"Aaaarrrgghh!" he bellowed, then stumbled and fell, holding his leaking flesh. "You shot me!"

"You thought I wouldn't?"

He was blowing air like a whale through its blow hole. "You bitch!"

Jazmine came over and squatted beside him, gun in hand. "I'm going to overlook that, because in this case, you're right. But we don't have much time, or should I say, *you* don't have much time. You know that Biggie song where he says, 'If you ain't got the clientele say hell no, because they gonna want their money rain, sleet, hail, snow,'" she snickered. "They, being the Cartel. Now, are you listening?"

His silent glare told her he was.

"This is the situation. Your nephew is dead. Your team is dead. Your man Big D will soon be dead, but I'm getting ahead of myself. Miss Toni works for me, Swag works for me, and now *you* work for me. Every shipment you receive, I get seventy percent of the profit, after you pay the Cartel, that is. They *never* know my name. You remain the face of this operation, but I'm the brains . . . and the balls," she added, unable to resist. "Any questions?"

"Go fuck yourself, bitch! Fish don't bow to no bitch! I'll tell the Cartel you took the coke!" he threatened.

"Little 'ol me?" she teased, batting her eyelashes. "A bitch killed your whole team, took your coke, and totally played you? If they believe you, they'll probably kill you for being so stupid. But hey, have it your way. I've got the Yayo" She winked.

She stood up and began to walk away. Kingfish gritted. The pain in his shoulder was nothing compared to the fear in his stomach of what the Cartel would do to him.

"Okay," he grumbled.

She stopped at the door. "You say something?"

"Okay, goddamn, okay!" he barked. "Now, call an ambulance. I'm fuckin' bleedin'!"

"In your situation, Kingfish, that's a good thing . . . now, one last point. Big D."

"What about him?"

"Kill him," Jazmine responded, looking him dead in the eyes. "We signed this contract in *his* blood."

Kingfish knew what she was doing. Big D was his last loyal soldier. She wanted to make sure he had no one and she had everyone.

"When do I get the coke back?"

"You don't. We'll move it. You're just the face, remember? And Fish . . . make sure Big D's body turns up for the police to find. Your word is worthless to me," she replied, then walked out.

-18-

"Oh yes, Daddy! Yessss!"

That was the first thing Jazmine heard as she knocked on Miss Toni's door. His cries of passion filled the apartment building's hallways as if his bed was right by the door. Jazmine knocked again, then called. Miss Toni picked up breathlessly.

"I know, I know, give me a minnnnn," he squealed before the line went dead.

Several minutes later, he answered the door in a robe, looking completely flustered.

"I told you I was on my way," Jazmine replied as she stepped inside.

"I told you I was too," Miss Toni sassed playfully.

The two shared a girlish giggle.

"I just came from Kingfish's. Besides having to shoot his fat ass, everything went smooth," Jazmine informed Miss Toni.

"Shoot him? Is he dead?"

Jazmine waved him off. "Flesh wound. He'll be fine."

Miss Toni stood and looked at Jazmine, shaking his head, admiringly.

"I can't believe it was so easy! Twenty million dollars! The only thing I had twenty-million of is problems!" Miss Toni laughed.

Jazmine joined her, then Miss Toni hugged her.

"It's amazing what a woman with a moustache can do, huh?" Jazmine jibed with a wink, then added, "So . . . where's the lucky dude?"

Miss Toni's smile got crooked. "Oh, he's just umm... a dude you know . . . ummm, nobody special," Miss Toni stammered.

"I'm sure I'm not his type, but the way you were screaming, I've *got* to see what he's working with," Jazmine snickered, then went straight to Miss Toni's bedroom door.

"Jazmine, wait!" he called out, but it was too late.

Jazmine opened the door. Lying on the bed, butt ass naked, was the little Morris Chestnut looking dude from the club. His dick was sticking straight up and was damn near taller than he was.

"Oh, you ready for some, mo—What!" he hollered, when he saw it wasn't Miss Toni. "Damn! Who are you?"

Jazmine's expression went sour as she looked at Miss Toni.

"Baby, let mother explain. I *really* intended to do as we talked about but look at all that! Mother really is in love!" Miss Toni exclaimed.

Jazmine looked at him, eyed his dick, then replied, "Yeah, you're right. It really is a shame to waste all that."

In one swift motion, she pulled her pistol and with one shot, lifted Morris's hair like he had a flip top head, and his brains jumped out and splattered the wall, the look of surprise frozen on his face forever.

With the gunshot echoing all over Miss Toni's amazement, Jazmine turned to him, her expression ice cold.

"I tell you to do something, you do it. I like to think I can trust you. Am I wrong?"

Miss Toni shook his dead.

"N–no."

"Good . . . it's still hard. Maybe you can get one more ride." Jazmine smirked, then turned and headed for the door.

It was right then that she decided to kill Miss Toni.

-19-

The water felt good to Bianca, despite the circumstances. For the first few days, she hadn't been allowed to take a shower. It was one of the many mind games Satan used to break young spirits. Now, standing under the warm, vigorous stream of water, she tried to block out the fact that there were several other females in the shower with her. It reminded her of the shower in the girls' locker room at school. The biggest difference being, there were now grown men ogling and molesting the girls at random.

Bianca kept her face forward, looking at the wall as she washed her body. She tried to block out the cries and sobs, the screams of pleasure and pain, the smell of sex in the air.

"It's not bad once you get used to it," Tammy told her after having been taken from the cage a third time.

Every night for the week she'd been there, the goons would cruise the cages pulling out girls as they pleased, some going kicking and screaming, others going willingly. Bianca would huddle in the farthest corner and wish herself invisible.

"Damn, lil' mama, how I miss *you*?"

Bianca heard the voice and it made her stiffen. She knew he was talking to her. She tried to ignore it and wash faster, hoping if she scrubbed hard enough and fast enough she could scrub herself clean away and rinse down the drain.

Then he put his hand on her naked shoulder.

"Hmmm, look at that tight little ass." He lusted. "I got to pop this cherry!" His hand traced down her back. She wanted to fight back, but she had seen what happened to those that did. As his hand traced lower and lower and lower on her back, she felt so alone, so abandoned, so helpless, so . . .

A hand grabbed his wrist right before he caressed Bianca's ass. He looked up. It was Alicia.

"Come on, baby, that pussy still green. She can't make her ass cum like I can," Alicia cooed in his ear, voice full of lust, but eyes as dead as a blind man's.

He licked his lips as he eyed Alicia's shapely frame. "I never seen a bitch ass cum before."

"Then let me pop *your* cherry." She giggled.

She took his hand and led him away. She looked back at Bianca. Her eyes may've been cold, but her heart surely wasn't.

Later that night, when the sandwiches had been passed out, Alicia came to Bianca's recessed corner of the cage and spoke to her through the fence.

"I brought you something," Alicia whispered, sliding a peanut butter sandwich under the bottom bar.

"Th–thank you," Bianca replied, quickly unwrapping the sandwich and devouring it almost whole.

They looked at each other while she chewed. Bianca wanted to thank her for what she had done earlier, but the thought of it all made her want to forget it totally.

Slowly, Alicia's smile melted.

"He . . . he's coming for you."

"Who?"

"Satan."

Bianca shivered. "You-you mean the devil?"

"No, not that devil, the *real* one, the one who brought you here," Alicia explained.

Bianca instantly knew who she was talking about. The albino man with the ghoulish eyes. Her whole body shuddered. "No, please God . . ." she prayed fervently.

"Listen, I know you're scared, but you *have* to be a good girl, okay? You *have* to obey him. It'll be better for you."

“No!”

“Shhhh!”

“No,” Bianca protested under her breath. “I have to get away. My daddy’s a policeman—he’ll help us. We can run away.”

Alicia shook her head. “We’ll never make it, he’ll find us. Besides, I-I don’t want to run away . . . I have no place to go,” Alicia said with the resignation of a slave.

“You can go with me! Please, just call my daddy! His number is—” Bianca started, but Alicia cut her off.

“Stop it! Just . . . *stop!*” she growled. “Your daddy can’t save you! No one can! You have to be good. Do you know what happens to these girls? They will be sold to very bad men all over the world, to places where they can’t speak the languages. No one can *hear* them then. Do you understand? Do you want to end up like that? Do you!”

“N–no,” Bianca stammered.

“Then stop being foolish. When he comes, *don’t resist*. Then you can be my little sister, okay?” Alicia said, caressing Bianca’s fingers on the gate, and looking at her like Aria once looked at her.

Bianca nodded. Tears flowing. Alicia stood up.

“I have to go. Don’t cry, little sister . . . you’ll soon be cleansed.”

-20-

The body of twenty-six-year-old Damien Bryant, also known as Big D, was found in the parking lot behind Dollar General. The deceased suffered two gunshot wounds and was located because he had fallen on the horn . . .

Jazmine smiled to herself. She didn't even have to read the rest of the newspaper article.

Mission accomplished. She had done all she had set out to do.

She and Swag had come to the Nola looking to start over, but circumstances made her have to start over alone. She could still smell his fresh blood as it oozed from his lifeless body.

"Je ne regrette rein," she had sang to him, one of his favorite songs. Over his dead body she had vowed to avenge him, but it took some time before she knew how. She knew who had done it. But Love had an army, and she was *only* one woman.

Then she realized that was more than enough.

At first, she had planned to become a cop to infiltrate their organization, but then she decided she would *take* their organization. That Halloween night, watching the kids transform themselves into ghosts and goblins . . . masks everywhere, masks on everyone. He may've been gone, but he lived on in her, and in the process, made her more of herself.

Thus, Swag was born, or better said, re-born.

The ring of her computer brought her back to the present. It had been running a query of the Matson's account. Matson had said their bank account had recently been hacked, and she knew that sometimes those kinds of events were linked. Identity thieves used the information for even more sinister crimes.

Jazmine looked at the screen and began scrolling through, looking at the fraudulent charges marked off in red . . . but that wasn't what caught her eyes. In fact, a few times she missed it, but the brain is trained to see patterns.

My Best Brother Mentoring Agency.

Over and over, there were similar deposits made into the account from the mentoring agency. She knew the agency well. She used to work there.

It was Love's mentoring agency.

"Son of a bitch!" she griped.

She scrolled back and back . . . and back. The deposits went back at least ten years. The amounts varied, never very large, sometimes a thousand, sometimes two, month after month after month.

Jazmine sat back, amazed.

"The motherfucka's been on the take the whole time!" she exclaimed. "No wonder Hall couldn't catch Love. He had Matson in his pocket!"

She hit print and waited for the reams and reams of evidence to spew from the printer.

Jazmine took the stack straight to his office. She couldn't wait to see the look on his by-the-book-face. The whole time he was after her, he was just as dirty as she was!

When she got to his office, he wasn't there. She asked another detective, "Hey Tomlin, you seen the boss?"

"Yeah, he went home about an hour ago."

Jazmine headed straight for her car, planning . . . scheming, how she would add him to the pawns on her board, but as she turned the key, it hit her . . .

Wait a minute . . .

If Matson had been on the take the whole time, why didn't he snitch her out to Love and let him know she was an undercover?

Something didn't add up, but she was damn sure about to find out why.

##########

Sonia lay on the bed in a semi-fetal position, almost catatonic. It had been a month since Bianca's abduction, and she was taking it extremely hard.

Why did I let her go to the bathroom by herself . . . all those people, anything could happen. . . I—I should've gone with her, held her hand. Oh God, please don't punish her for my sins! Her thoughts screamed, as the tears streamed down her cheeks.

"Baby . . . I brought you some soup," Matson announced gently, as he entered the room.

He set the bowl down on the night table and sat on the bed looking at his wife. It hurt so bad to see her hurt and to feel like there was nothing he could do. The whole department had rallied behind him, but it was like she had disappeared.

Matson brushed back the hair from her face and caressed her cheek.

"I'm—I'm sorry," Sonia whispered so softly, it broke Matson's heart.

"Baby, noooooo," he replied, getting down on his knees in front of her and hugging her tight. "Nooo, this wasn't your fault," he added, his mind saying, *It was mine.*

He felt like God was punishing him, reminding him of his awesome power. That his lack of discretion had somehow been visited on the next generation.

"But you have to eat. We'll find her, I promise, but I need you to be strong, okay?" he urged.

Sonia slowly nodded. He helped her sit up, then spoon for spoon, he fed her the soup. She looked at him.

"Why are you so good to me?"

Matson smiled. "Because you look like Gabrielle Union," he joked.

She laughed through her tears. "She wasn't even a star when we met."

"Then you know it's because I love you."

"I love you, too."

They hugged tightly, warmly, meaningfully, like two lovers on the deck of the Titanic before the . . .

Ding dong!

They broke the hug.

"Who is it, Tony?" she asked, anxiety creeping into her voice. "Oh my God, what if…"

He didn't even want her to give the words wings. He hugged her again.

"Shh, shh, it's not. It's not. I'll get it. Just relax, okay?"

He went downstairs and answered the door.

It was Jazmine. His jaw line hardened.

"What do you want?"

"We have to talk."

"Can't it wait?"

"No."

"Well, it will," he spat back, and began to shut the door.

"Did you make Love wait?" she retorted as the door closed.

He opened it again. Confusion and annoyance all over his expression.

"What?"

"Like I said, we need to talk," Jazmine reiterated.

"About?"

"You and Love."

"Talk."

A wicked smirk colored her expression.

"You really wanna open the closet in the middle of the street?"

He had no idea what she was talking about, but her vibe compelled him to step aside, allowing her in.

Jazmine entered. He closed the door. She was carrying a thick stack of print outs that she let hit the coffee table like a stack of newspapers.

"So, it was you the whole time, huh?"

"Me what?" Matson replied, baffled.

He definitely wasn't acting like a man who had something to hide. She picked up half the stack and handed it to him.

"It's highlighted in yellow."

He looked, eyes scanning up and down the columns.

"My Best Brother Mentoring Agency? Okay, *and*?" he questioned.

"That's a record of your bank account. All of those amounts are deposits, going back ten years, and you're telling me you don't know *anything* about that?" Jazmine questioned intently.

"I'm a cop, Coleman, and a damn good one. I've never had any improper relations with Love. Can you say the same?" Matson shot back.

She ignored the implications and replied, "Well, who else would have access to . . . "

Her voice trailed off as words seemed to bring both of them to the same realization. Jazmine's gaze became embarrassed for him, while his just . . . glazed over.

"I'll look into it, "he finally said, breaking the awkward silence.

Jazmine left the printouts on the coffee table and walked out. Matson just stared at the sheets of incriminating papers.

There was only one other person with access to the account. Sonia.

His heart refused to believe what his head knew had to be true. He scooped up the printouts and went upstairs. When he entered; Sonia looked at him.

"Tell me about Terrance Love."

The look on her face told him everything he needed to know.

########

Satan stood behind Aria, stroking her hair as she sat at her vanity table. They looked at each other through the mirror.

"You're beautiful," he remarked.

"Thank you," Aria replied.

She was wearing only a thong and a bra, applying her makeup as she got ready to go out with him to the Jazz Ensemble.

He ran his hand over her neck, then down inside her bra, caressing her nipple until it hardened in his hand. Aria's eyelids fluttered.

"We're going to be late," she whispered, temperature rising. He slid the straps of her bra and slip to the side until her breasts popped free. Her breathing intensified. Satan bent and licked the length of her neck,

sliding his hands down her sides until he pushed his fingers inside her pussy.

"Ohhh," she cooed, opening her legs and grinding against his fingers.

"This pussy stay wet," he groaned into her ear, pulling her up and bending her over until she could damn near kiss her own reflection.

Satan slid his dick in her tight pussy with a grunt, filling her with his girth and making her cry out.

"Daddy!"

He gripped her by the hips and began long dicking her strong and hard, watching the fuck faces she was making in the mirror.

"Whose pussy is this!" he gruffed.

"Yours!" Aria squealed; the sound of his slapping thrusts just as loud as her moans.

He slid two fingers in her asshole and began fingering her to the same rhythm of his strokes.

"Oh Da–Daddy, my pussy is on fire!"

She watched her own reflection in the mirror, seeing the intensity of each stroke in her facial expression. Love and hate, pain and pleasure mixed as her body grew hotter and hornier.

"It feels so good!" she sang.

"Tell me!"

"I love you!"

"Tell me again!"

"Oh, I love youuuuu!"

She knew he was about to cum. She cocked her leg up on her bench and threw the pussy back hard. His body jerked twice, then she felt the warm spurt of his seed coat her walls.

Catching his breath, he leaned over, kissed her on her neck and said, "I love you . . . remember that."

He said it like a warning.

Their eyes locked in the mirror, before he pulled out of her and added, "Get dressed."

##########

The limo pulled up to the cultural center, a large glass-like structure that sat in the middle of downtown New Orleans like a crown jewel. Many of the city's luminaries were out, including Mayor Ray Nagin. Satan, the pastor of one of the oldest churches in the city was a major patron of the arts, so everyone knew he would be there . . .

Everyone.

Even the homeless man on the side of the street. No one paid attention to him. No one even put a coin in the empty soup can that sat beside him. He lay there, his dreams covering his face, his oversized army coat covering his body. He looked like a clump of garbage.

Aria stepped out of the limo in a shimmering satin gown that seemed to leave glitter in her wake. Her long hair was done up in an upsweep that gave her a royal air. Satan stepped out behind her in an immaculate white tuxedo and gold cummerbund. The goons, in black tuxedos, all four of them, kept their eyes peeled like the secret service.

But no one ever pays attention to the homeless.

As Aria, on Satan's arm, stepped past the neglected lump, he rose up so swiftly that he seemed to appear out of nowhere. He grabbed her wrist with one hand and opened fire with a small body Mac .11, spitting automatic rounds into the chest of two of the goons.

Thump! Thump! Thump! Thump!

Over the sounds of the street as each bullet blew through the bodies, spewing blood everywhere.

"What the fuck!"

It took the other two half a minute to realize the homeless man wasn't a homeless man, but their worst nightmare. By the time they drew their weapons, he had Aria in front of him like a shield and the Mac .11 to her head. They aimed. Satan looked into his cold green and gray eyes. 'If I can't have her, no one will,' they seemed to say.

"Don't shoot!" he gritted, talking to his goons.

"Oh my God!" Aria cried.

"Shut up!" Swag hissed. "Put them down, now!"

The goons hesitated.

"Do as he says," Satan ordered, his jaw muscles flexing.

Everything had happened so fast; the rest of the crowd hadn't had time to react.

"Oh my!"

"They're shooting!"

Swag began to back away, dragging Aria along.

"Please don't do this," she begged.

"Don't say another word," Swag warned.

His eyes never left Satan's.

"You sure you want to do this? Let her go and you can walk away clean," Satan offered.

"I'm telling you the same thing," Swag retorted, then disappeared around the corner.

As soon as he was out of sight, he put the nozzle of the gun under her chin.

"Run or die!"

She ran, with his hand around hers. His motorcycle was only a car length ahead. When he got to it, he let the Mac .11 fall from his gloved hand, produced a leather strap and barked, "Get on!"

She did it without hesitation. In one smooth motion he wrapped the strap around her waist and his, fastened it, kick started the bike and said, "Try anything, I kill us both!" he spat, and from the look in his eyes, she knew he was serious.

As soon as Swag and Aria bent the corner, the two goons scooped their guns off the pavement and took off after them. As soon as they came around the corner, Swag and Aria were roaring off on the bike. They took aim but Satan stopped them.

"No . . . you can only hit her," he warned them, his coal black eyes enflamed, "Don't worry . . . I know where he's going."

-21-

It seemed they were riding for hours. The cold wind whipping across her bare shoulders had her teeth chattering.

"Where are we going?" she yelled, the wind snatching most of the sound away.

He didn't respond. It was too cold to lift her head again. His back shielded her from the wind. She put her head against him then went to sleep.

##########

The cessation of movement made her open her eyes, but it was so dark she thought they were still closed. In the minute it took for her eyes to adjust, her nose already had. She smelled a familiar earthy but pungent aroma.

The bayou.

The sounds all around let her know the swamp was alive. The only thing man made was a small plank house that sat in a clearing to her left. The cedar wood looked worn; what was once brown now appeared to be a grayish color. A porch surrounded the front of the house supported by stilts that lifted it above the water. She could make out the faint glow of candles burning inside, but other than that, the house was totally dark.

"Why did you do this? You don't understand . . . Please, you must take me back!" Aria begged but tried to sound firm.

"No," Swag replied, eyeing her reaction.

"Fuck you! Take me back now!"

He smirked. "You want to go . . . go."

She wanted to smack the smirk off his face, but the situation was too serious for distractions.

"I'm gone!" she shouted, then turned and stormed off.

She almost twisted her ankles twice. The bayou was no place for six-inch stilettos. The third time it happened, she snatched off her shoes and flung them in frustration.

The next step made her wish she hadn't.

The terra of the bayou is always squishy and moist. She felt like she was walking on a slimy sponge, squirting gooey slime all between her toes, up to her ankles.

She stepped over a fallen log. A low-hanging vine almost clotheslined her . . . but vines don't hiss.

She froze.

The vine, or what she thought was a vine, uncoiled and lowered its head until it was eyes to eyes with her. It was the biggest snake she had ever seen. If it were to open its mouth, it seemed it could swallow her whole.

Sssssssssss!

It hissed. Its forked tongue damn near touching the tip of her nose.

"Don't move," Swag warned her, "but don't be afraid either. His tongue can taste fear, and if it does, it will strike."

Aria stared into its reptilian eyes. It reminded her of a cat's eye. She had never been so scared in her life, but she refused to show it. This is how she learned how to master her fear . . . she had no choice.

She looked the snake in the eyes and didn't flinch. The snake's pupils narrowed, then morphed into a diamond shape as if testing her resolve. But she decided, if it struck or not, she wouldn't show fear.

Slowly, it dropped to the ground, hissed, then slithered between her feet, brushing her ankle, then disappeared in the darkness.

Swag stepped up, smiling. "You've got heart."

"Yep," she replied, right before her eyes rolled in the back of her head and she passed out.

##########

"You shouldn't have brought her here."

"Let him come."

"It's not him . . . it's her."

"I don't understand."

Aria's opened eyes ended the conversation. She looked up and saw Swag talking to an old woman. Her face was a shadow, only dimly lit by the candle, but Aria could see she had long gray dreads that hung almost to her feet, and she had the same mis-matched eyes as Swag.

As soon as her eyes opened, their conversation ended. The old woman turned and walked out of the bedroom, closing the door behind her, and taking the candle with her.

In the room almost completely darkened, she could hear Swag breathing, smelled his presence. It excited and scared her at the same time. She jumped up.

"She's right. You have to take me back," Aria tried to demand, but it came out sounding like a plea.

"I never go back."

He stepped closer. She drew back, away, her back met the wall. She could run no farther. His hand traced the curve of her shoulder.

"If – if I give you some, will you take me home then?" she asked, sounding like an inquisitive little girl.

She heard him laugh for the first time, and it made her smile in the dark.

"You are home," he replied, then covered her mouth with his.

She had been wanting to taste him ever since he watched her fuck the senator. She had felt him behind her, and she half hoped that he'd snatch her up and fuck her himself. It was the same way in the church. Now that she was finally getting what she wanted, she couldn't see him. Only feel him. It was like the darkness itself had grown hands, and a tongue and a long, thick dick.

Swag didn't even bother to take off her dress, he just pulled it up, slid her panties to the side and slammed every inch of himself he could get inside her. Her back arched as if she had spasmed; her mouth hung open until the scream finally caught up.

". . . Ahhhhhhhhh!" she gasped.

He moaned deep in his throat as if he had never felt anything so good. Hearing his pleasure mitigated her pain and made her wrap her legs around his waist and throw that pussy back at him hard.

"Just like that, show me you're a big girl," he grunted.

"You li-like that? Is it good to you?" Aria spoke breathlessly.

*Swag beat the pussy like, if she hadn't have given it to him, he would've taken it. The headboard beat a steady rhythm, percussion to her high-pitched song. Her body began to tremble. It scared her. Satan had been fucking her since she was eleven, but she had never had an orgasm. Her twenty-something*year-old kidnapper was fucking her in ways her forty-two-year-old "teacher" never could. The sex felt good with Satan, but never felt right. Her body always resisted. But now, she felt something she never felt before.*

"Ohhhh myyy Gooddd!" She squeezed, digging her nails in his back. Her legs spasmed and wouldn't stop shaking as her pussy exploded, making him explode as well.

"Wait . . . please. Don't . . . move." She trembled, her body rigid with unbearable pleasure.

Swag then slowly undressed her, kissing and licking every inch of her body, making her cum two more times simply from the tip of his tongue.

"Don't . . . stop," she whispered, and when he slid into her the second time, it was like a marriage. Her body would forever be his.

########

*"You must take me back. He'll kill her if you don't,"
Aria told him the next morning.*

*The bedroom had no windows, so it was still dark.
The only light came from the sun seeping through the
cracks between the plank board walls. It reminded her
of a slave shack.*

"Kill who?" he asked.

She sat up, pulling her knees to her chest.

"My—my mother," she answered.

"I kidnapped you. He can't blame you."

"But he will. You don't know Daddy."

"He's not your daddy."

She looked at him. "How do you know?"

*"Because, he wouldn't use you like he did," Swag
replied, caressing her sweaty back. It was so humid in
the bayou she woke up sweating.*

*Aria blew a chuckle. "He says that sex is a woman's
greatest weapon. He is teaching me to use it well."*

"Then he is your teacher."

"And Daddy."

*"Stop calling him that," Swag snarled, sitting up
beside her.*

"Why?" she inquired.

"Because he is not your father . . . he's mine."

Their eyes met and her voice caught in her throat, but looking into his eyes, she could see the coal blackness in them.

He caressed her cheek. "How old were you when he stole you?" he asked softly.

Aria shook her head and looked away. He turned her face back to his in time to see the first tear fall.

"He—he didn't steal me . . . my mother gave me away," she admitted.

Saying the words made her break down into sobs. He gathered her up into his arms and held her tight, feeling her tears drench his shoulders.

"She . . . she wanted to be an opera singer. Satan said he . . . he would help make her a star, on one condition . . . if she gave him me," she cried. "I ran away at first. I was nine when he caught me. He said if I ever ran away again, he'd—he'd kill her."

Swag pulled back to look into her eyes.

"But you didn't run away this time."

"In my heart I did," she replied, the look in her eyes saying she was exactly where she wanted to be. She just felt guilty about being there.

He nodded, then stood and paced the floor.

"Your mother . . . does he know where she is?"

"Yes. She lives in New York."

"Then I will take care of her for you," he vowed.

Aria got up and hugged his neck. A look passed between them, then she kissed him greedily.

"What about Satan?"

Swag scoffed. "Don't call him that either. All he is, is what he's always been. The pastor."

"Why do they call him Satan?"

"A name they gave him in Vietnam, because when he was around, death was assured," he explained, thinking to himself, the apple doesn't fall far from the tree.

"When will you go to New York?"

"Tonight."

"I want to go with you."

"No. Stay here . . . believe me." He smirked. "It won't take long."

##########

Miranda Lemieux was one of the few black opera singers in the world, therefore, whenever they wanted to add a splash of color to an event, they rang her phone. She had performed all over the world, her most famous rendition being 'Carmen,' especially since she looked like Lena Horne.

The theatre was packed for her performance. It may've been off Broadway, but the black tie was still a requirement.

Except for the nun.

She moved through the crowd, keeping her head down, her rosary beads in hand, mumbling Hail Mary's.

"That nun has some rather large hands," one woman casually remarked in passing, but thought nothing of it until later . . . much later.

Her performance was exquisite. A lyric soprano, Miranda's voice filled the space like the smell of spring in a garden. After hearing her, no one would be able to hear another lyric soprano without comparison.

Throughout the performance, the nun sat for all three hours, never lifting her gaze from the rosary beads. No one thought it strange that a nun attended an opera. Priests attended all the time. In fact, it was rumored that Miranda had even performed for the Pope himself. So, a nun's presence was truly a sign.

When the performance ended, cries of "Encore!" resounded through the theatre. Miranda bowed gracefully and exited stage right.

Many gathered to shake her hand, or ask for an autograph, or to hand her a rose, but they all split like the Red Sea when the nun came forward. No one wanted to get in the way of Miranda's blessing . . .

Lucky them.

Miranda saw the sister coming and smiled ecstatically, her expression holding just the right amount of humility. The nun walked into her embrace, right up to her ear, and in a language she hadn't heard in so long, a language she had tried to forget but hadn't, said, "This . . . is for your daughter."

Before she could react, the nun lifted her head and Miranda looked into the green-gray glare that froze her in her spot. She opened her mouth to scream. Swag grabbed her by the jaw hard, making her tongue stick out. With the other latex-covered hand, he held a scalpel. He brought it down swiftly on her tongue, severing half of it in one bloody swipe. Before the chunk of flesh hit the ground, he brought the scalpel across her eyes and the bridge of her nose, slitting her corneas and blinding her for life. The red blood running from her face made her look like a cyborg.

It all happened so fast.

Zzzzippp – zzzzippp!

That she was already blinded by the time the crowd began to scream and backpedal.

"Oh my God!"

"Look!"

Miranda tried to scream but couldn't. Without a tongue, she could only gurgle her panic. Her bodyguard moved in much too late.

Boc! Boc!

Two shots exploded one of the bodyguards' chest and started the whole lobby stampeding.

"Gun!"

Swag dipped off quickly, merging in the crowd just as house security began to search desperately for the nun. He shed the nun's habit; underneath he was dressed in a tuxedo. He snatched off the gloves, took a pair of glasses out of his pocket and put them on, becoming as mild mannered as Clark Kent.

When he came around the corner, screaming and running all around him, he ran into security.

"The nun! The nun! Have you seen the nun?" one asked.

"No, no, I speak no English," he mumbled in French.

The two guards ran off, in pursuit of their own tail while the real dog walked away scot free.

##########

The old woman made Aria uncomfortable.

She refused to speak to Aria, not even returning her greetings of good morning for all three days Swag was gone. She remembered what the old woman had said when she had first come.

"It's not him . . . it's her."

Aria wanted to know what she meant.

The nights were the worst.

Lying in the pitch-black darkness, Aria swore she could hear the whispering in the wind. Sometimes the voices said her name. She knew enough about voodoo not to answer, but the words still chilled her even though it was so hot, the slightest movement made her sweat. She would curl up, knowing she could hear the slither of snakes on the floorboard.

The only time the old woman acknowledged her presence was when it was time to eat.

"Come," she would grumble.

On the fourth morning, she heard Swag's motorcycle pull up outside. She forgot all about her grumbling stomach and ran outside to greet him.

Aria jumped in his arms and covered his face with kisses.

"I missed you! Did you see my mother? Is she okay? Did you take care of her?" she asked, her voice as light as a child.

Swag set her down and handed her the newspaper.

"I told you I would."

She looked at the newspaper. The headline read:

OPERA SINGER ATTACKED.

She read until she knew enough. That an attacker dressed as a nun had cut out her mother's tongue and blinded her permanently.

. . . The police have no suspects.

But Aria did. She was looking at him.

"You . . . did this to my mother?" she hissed, her voice trembling with strong emotion.

"She stopped being your mother when she sold you. Now that she is blind, she will see that," Swag replied.

Aria dropped the paper and lunged wildly at Swag, her punches landing on his face. Her nails digging into his neck.

"I can't believe you did this to me! I hate you!" she screamed as she was determined to hit, scratch, and hurt him in any way that she could.

Swag allowed her to vent her emotions on him, casually blocking some and allowing other blows to land. Feeling her tire, he pulled her into his embrace and held her tightly.

"It had to be done. Everyone must be held accountable one day. Besides, I also saved her life. He won't kill her now," Swag consoled her.

Deep down, Aria knew he was right. For years, she had kept the hatred of her mother bottled up inside of her love. The day her mother walked away, ignoring her cry, killed something inside her. She wanted her mother to hurt like she hurt, but she could've never brought herself to do it. Now that Swag had, it bonded her to him for life.

-22-

Matson felt like someone had pulled the rug out from under his whole life. Nothing or no one was who they seemed. Here was his wife, his beautiful, loving wife of nine years, who wasn't really his wife at all.

"I . . . I don't know what else to say, Tony. I'm sorry," Sonia sobbed, her heart broken for him.

She knew he was a good man. He didn't deserve what she had done, but not even God could change the past.

"The whole time . . . the whole time," he whispered, shaking and rubbing his head. "Why Sonia . . . *why*?"

The anguish in his voice was killing her.

"I–I have no excuse, Tony. I could say I was lonely, with you always gone, or –or, the fact that . . . he gave me things, things we couldn't afford, things . . . when times were hard," she admitted, trying to finally come clean.

He looked up at her, wearing an unbearable expression.

"When was the last time?"

She dropped her head, ashamed to answer.

"When, Sonia?" he stressed.

". . .A month before he died," she whispered hoarsely.

"A month?" he echoed, then he chuckled. "A fuckin' *month* . . . don't you see what he was doin', you stupid *bitch*? He was using you! Using you to pick your brain about me!"

Sonia covered her face crying.

"I see that now! The way he–he always asked about cases you were working on. I'm sorry, Tony. I thought he loved me!"

"Loved *you*! I thought you loved *me*! How could you do this to me, Sonia? *How*!" Tony spat, standing up to pace.

He thought of all the nights he would casually talk to her about cases. He thought her questions were genuine interest, not the puppet strings being pulled from afar.

"So, you were going to leave me for this menace?" he barked.

"No," she lied, reverting back to her secret self.

The truth was she didn't know. But now that Love was dead, she wasn't about to give up her bird in the hand. Besides, she did love Tony, too.

Matson walked up to the bed, looked down and into her eyes.

"Is Bianca even mines? Hell, what about Felecity? Is *she* mine?"

The last thing Matson remembered was Sonia crying, then looking up and saying, "I don't know."

He blacked out, but he didn't pass out. He was conscious of not being fully conscious. Conscious of his heart beating hard and fast, anger and pain coursing through his pumping veins, through every artery, until it exploded, blowing him out of the darkness and back into reality.

When he came to, the room was wrecked. The mirror was broken, the chair overturned, and the lamp was smashed. The room looked like a hurricane had blown through, and in the middle of the floor lay Sonia. Her panties were ripped, her nightgown up over her titties. Her left eye was swollen, and her pussy was oozing cum.

Matson looked down and found his pants around his ankles and his hard dick covered with the juice of her sex.

"You didn't have to say those things, Tony," she cried, her ribs feeling sore.

"What things?" he asked, his mind still trying to remember the blackout.

All she could do was curl up and cry.

Matson slowly stood up and stumbled out, leaving Sonia to contemplate how it had all come down to this...

########

He stopped talking and just danced. She loved to dance. Music had always played a big part in her life. Tony didn't dance. He didn't go to clubs. But being able to dance again made her juices flow. It wasn't like she was trying to dance nasty; it was just what the music did to her.

Kev, picking up on her vibe, danced closer. At first it was cool, until he started riding her ass with his hard dick.

She stepped away, then turned to face him.

"Umm, you're dancing kind of close."

Kev smiled. "Just tryin' to show you what you do to me."

"Huh?"

He pulled her to him to repeat himself, but she snatched away and stopped dancing.

"Excuse you."

"Come on, sexy lady. Throwin' that ass like that, I know you want it. What a nigguh gotta do? Pay?" he yelled, pulling out a wad of money.

"Fuck you!" she spazzed, then started to storm off.

He grabbed her arm, embarrassed to be screamed on.

"Bitch, who is you talkin' to like that?" his words bellowed.

"Bitch? Yo' mama is a bitch!" she spat back.

Kev jerked her hard. "Bitch, I'ma—" he seethed, drawing back his hand.

"You what?"

Kev heard the masculine voice. He looked, ready to beef, until he saw who it was.

"Love! My nig—"

"Yo, fam', if you got a problem with your lady, take her home. Don't be disrespectin' my club with that bullshit," Love roared over the music.

"I'm not with him!" Sonia spat, looking at Love, her mind screaming, 'Tyson Beckford!'

Love looked at Kev.

"Naw, Love, I wouldn't diss you, yo. My bad, Love, on the real," Kev stammered, copping a plea.

Sonia had never known a man who commanded respect with just a glance. Instantly, she was intrigued.

"You okay, ma?" Love asked.

She nodded, not trusting her voice.

He turned to Kev. "Keep it movin', yo."

Kev bounced with the quickness. Love turned to walk away. Before Sonia even realized it herself, she blurted out, "Excuse me."

Love stopped and looked back. She was stuck. Pinned by his gaze, not knowing what else to say, she said, ". . .Thank you."

Love smiled and replied, "No doubt, ma . . . who are you here with?"

"Huh?" she said, even though she could hear him under the music. His voice seemed to be that deep. She just wanted him to backtrack. He did, leaned in close to her ear and said, "I said . . . who are you here with?"

Damn it seemed as if every word dripped in her ear, then trickled its way lower . . .

"My–my, ummm–girlfriends."

As soon as she stuttered, he knew he had her.

"You think you and your girlfriends would like to have a drink with me and my peoples?"

She blushed. "I'll ask them."

"You do that."

As soon as Mimi saw who she was talking about, Sonia swore she saw her eyeballs roll like slot machines and come up with dollar signs. Ka–ching!

"Girl, that is Love himself! The nigguh that owns this club and this city! A drink? I'll dance on the table!"

Katira and Sonia laughed.

"Shit, why not? Lead the way!" Katira chimed in.

Love led them up to his office. The glasses were double thick, so the club sounded like a muffled thud below. Antman and Thump were waiting for them to come. As soon as Mimi laid eyes on Ant she pushed up, leaving Katira with Thump.

Love gave Sonia her drink.

"Now that we can talk without yelling, I'm Love," he charmed.

They shook hands, with Love holding her hand an extra beat. He had already peeped her engagement ring, but he had also seen the gleam in her eyes. She was like a goldfish being circled by a shark . . .

"He's a very lucky man," Love complimented.

"Thank you." She smiled, the third drink taking effect.

"But lucky only wins you the prize . . . it can't help you keep it."

The laughter and drinks flowed. Love knew he'd never get her to leave with him, so he did the next best thing. He texted Thump and Ant:

Get them bitches outta here.

Ant made his move first.

"What up, ma? You tryin' to bounce with me or what?"

"Shit, daddy, you already know," she replied lustfully.

Katira was a little more reluctant; she knew the nigguh may've been ugly, but his money wasn't.

"Are you sure you're going to be okay?" Katira asked Sonia.

"Ma, don't worry. I'll make sure she gets home safe," Love assured her. Once they were alone, Love wasted no time going in for the kill.

"Are you ready to leave?"

"I–I really should . . ."

He took that as a no.

He poured.

She drank.

As soon as she finished it, he pulled her body to him. The swiftness of the move startled her, but he could see right through her good girl mask.

"Love, I—"

"He treats you like a queen, doesn't he? Holds the door when you walk through? Covers your body with soft kisses and all that, but I bet that nigguh ain't never just fucked you like a nasty bitch, ever," Love growled in her ear, the whole time his hands smacking and

squeezing her ass, inching up her skirt until nothing but ass and thighs fell out.

Sonia squirmed, but she didn't fight. Every word went right to her pussy, and when he said, 'nasty bitch,' she was ready to jump on his dick and go buck. No man had been so disrespectful and sexy. It sparked her like a flame. He slid three fingers in her sloppy wet pussy and bent her over the desk, fingering her furiously.

"Oh–oh–oh yessss," she sang, grinding his fingers.

"You like that, don't you? I'ma beat this pussy until you cum all over my dick, then make you lick it up," Love grunted, dropping his pants and slamming his hard, thick dick up in her.

"Yes, daddy, whatever you want," she panted.

Love grabbed a handful of her hair, pulling her head back and smacking her chocolate ass, red.

"Oh God, you fuck me so good, so good." Sonia trembled.

Smack!

"That nigguh should see his queen now, taking. All. This. Dick. Like a nasty bitch!"

"Oh, I'm a nasty—"

Smack! Smack!

"Bitch!" she exploded, cumming harder than she ever had. True to his word, he pulled his crème-covered dick out and turned her around. Sonia fell to her knees *and gobbled him up with a long slurp. The taste of her own juices made her want to fuck again and again and again...*

That night, Love beat that pussy sore. He didn't drop her off until the sun broke the horizon.

Sonia was hooked.

After that, when Tony held a door for her, or pulled out her chair, she thought about Love coming to her job and fucking her in the bathroom. Whenever Tony covered her body with soft, wet kisses, she squirmed, feeling Love's hands around her throat, choking the shit out of her when she came.

"Love!" she cried out, but it was Tony's dick making her climax. Her whole body tensed, but Tony thought she was calling him 'my love.'

"I love you, too," Tony replied, kissing her passionately.

"Love—Love—Love, it's toooo biggggg!" she groaned.

"Shut up!" Love gruffed, sliding his big dick in her tight ass, inch by agonizingly pleasurable inch.

Her back spasmed. It felt like his shaft was in her spine. She had never been fucked in her ass. The first time it hurt, but once Love popped her cherry, she begged for it.

"Daddy, put it in my assssss, cum in my ass!"

Her heart was with Tony, but her body craved Love. She was literally torn.

Until she found out she was pregnant.

She used one of those home pregnancy tests. She did it in the bathroom in Tony's apartment, thinking he was asleep. He wasn't. When he walked in and saw her holding the blue stick, his eyes got big.

"Baby! Tell me I'm seeing blue!" he exclaimed, squinting at the stick.

Tears flowed, but she was too choked up to speak. He ran over and took the stick out of her hand.

"Oh my God! I'm gonna be a daddy!" he exclaimed excitedly, snatching her off her feet.

She couldn't bear to tell him. Even though technically it could've been his, she knew it wasn't. A woman knows. The blood test would later confirm it was Love's. But she knew Love wasn't the type of man she could spend her life with. She decided right then; Tony could never know.

When she told Love, he took it well.

"Baby, I'll always be there for mine," he vowed, and he was.

He gave her Dolla sometimes, but he wanted to keep a paper trail as well, in case she ever got on some child support shit. He also kept her straight. Love was the one who bought those new designer shoes. Love was the only one who helped her cop the BMW. Whenever Tony would question an influx of sudden money, Sonia would always say, "I borrowed it from my parents."

Then Love had to do three years in the Feds.

A part of Sonia was relieved. The double life was beginning to get to her. But the other part of her, the wild part of her, missed the dick downs Love would put on her.

Until.

"Love! You're home? Why did you come here? Someone might see you!" Sonia gasped, scared, excited and suddenly horny at the same time. He came straight to her house.

##########

A parade of young, trembling flesh disgraced the stage. Some being sold alone, others, in pairs and groups. They brought Satan hundreds of thousands of dollars before he even took a break to drink water. Bianca, naked and unashamed, brought him the glass on stage. Her young body made Satan's buzzer go crazy. He laughed.

"I'm sorry, gentlemen, my lady, but she is not for sale. She is one of mine. Isn't that right, child?"

"Yes . . . daddy," she replied, fighting hard to keep the disgust out of her voice. She knew her total obedience was needed to keep Tammy from being sold.

She left the stage, head high to tilt back the tears. It had been a month since she had been taken and each day her ability to forget what was and accept what *is* grew stronger. But her resolve never stopped the tears.

The next to come to the stage was a group of six girls, none younger than nine or older than twelve. They huddled close together, scared and helpless.

"Here I have the freshest, most tender pieces money can buy. Untampered with and ready to be . . . used," Satan remarked. "I open the bid at five hundred thousand."

There were instantly several bids. The numbers climbed up to one million quickly.

"I have one point two, do I have point three?" Satan requested.

Communications buzzed. He clicked in.

"Por favor, may I have a minute of your time?"

"Certainly," Satan answered.

He descended the stage and approached one of the compartments. As soon as he reached the door, it was opened by a large, muscular Mexican in a suit that barely covered the tattoos all over his neck and hands.

In the chair sat a Mexican who was known to the world as El Gordo but should've been called Jabba the Hut. He was as big as a whale. He labored just to breathe. Making it grotesque just to watch.

"I would offer you a drink, but it's *your* bar!" El Gordo huffed, ending in a hoarse laugh.

Satan sat in the opposite chair.

"Yes, but you can pour scotch and water."

The bodyguard fixed the drink then brought it to Satan.

"I will pay the top price, but . . . I have a slight problem," El Gordo explained.

"Which is?"

"Very recently, a very large shipment of mine was stolen. Not *from* me, you understand, but it is still *mine*. It is the principle, no?" El Gordo explained.

Satan nodded. El Gordo continued.

"The man who was robbed is named Kingfish. Very loyal, very reliable. His port of entry is very important to my coastal operations. If it can happen once, it can happen again!"

"I understand. You would like my people to eliminate the problem."

"Yes, yes, matalos!" El Gordo barked. "See Kingfish. He is known in this city. Solve this problem and I will be . . . very grateful."

Satan sipped his scotch. "I will take care of it . . . now." Satan smiled, "You may complete the transaction."

-23-

Matson drove in a bubble of blurs. Stop lights, people, cars, trees, blobs of scenes congealed outside, but he didn't recognize them. He didn't even know where he was going . . . until he got there.

As he sat looking at the door, he knew he should've called. Matson didn't know what he'd find. He definitely didn't want to see Jazmine. He wasn't ready for that yet. But he needed to talk to someone, and the Google map in his mind led him to Rain's doorstep.

He glanced up at the moon, absentmindedly thinking about all the times he and Sonia shared. Who they were was part of who he was. Now, finding out that it had all been a lie, he didn't know what truth was anymore.

Matson started to get out but decided to call first.

"Hello, you," she answered happily on the second ring.

Her warm welcome made his broken heart feel good.

"Hey, how are you?"

"You okay?" she asked, voice concerned.

Her concern felt as good as her welcome.

"Just . . . wanted to know if you wanted some company?" Matson asked, prepping himself for her to say no.

"Sure. I ummm, I'm just reading to my daughter. How long before you get here?"

He chuckled.

"Actually, I'm right outside," he replied and tooted his horn so she could hear.

She snickered.

"Oh," she started to ask why, but she remembered the game they were both playing. "Well, in that case, come on in!"

He hung up, and then remembered the GPS chip. Now would be a perfect time to plant it. Even in his funk, he still thought like a cop, and if the dude riding that bike wasn't Swag, who was he?

He took the tiny chip out of the glove box and put it in his pocket. Rain appeared in the door. The way the backlight shined through the oversized T-shirt, he saw the outline of her naked body underneath. Matson felt slowed down, but his dick seemed to grab itself, pulling him forward, like, 'nigguh come on!'

"Hey, sexy. How are you? I just have one more chapter to read, and then we can—" She looked up and down suggestively, then came back to his eyes. "Talk."

Rain shut the door behind him.

"That's cool. You mind if I get something to drink?"

"No, no, help yourself."

She went into Malaya's room while he went in the kitchen. Matson looked over his shoulder then quickly went over to the motorcycle. He applied the GPS chip's magnetic back to the underside of the seat. He knew someone not looking for it wouldn't notice it. He grabbed a glass, filled it with tap water, then walked in the back, following the sound of Rain's voice until he reached Malaya's room.

She was lying next to Malaya, holding open a big colorful book, reading. He leaned against the door and took in the scene with mixed emotions. It reminded him of Sonia and how she read to his girls.

His girls . . .

The thought ripped his heart and boiled his blood. They weren't *his* girls any more than the little girl Rain was reading to. The thought and cold reality of it all made his stomach drop. He was sick.

"Mommy, who's that?" Malaya pointed at Matson.

"Tony, Malaya, and what I tell you about pointing?"

"He's cuuute." Malaya giggled.

Rain laughed.

Matson chuckled.

"Go to sleep with your fast self."

Rain kissed her, then tucked her in.

"Good night, Mommy. I love you!"

"I love you, too." Rain hadn't expected him to come into Malaya's bedroom; she would have preferred for Malaya not to be there when he was in the house. But he caught her off guard, and she knew she needed to keep him close in order to get in his head.

Rain and Matson settled in the living room. She went in the kitchen, then came out with two wine glasses and a bottle of strawberry champagne.

"What are we celebrating?" Matson asked as she poured.

His feelings were a thousand miles from celebration.

"Well." She broke off his pour and poured hers. "Whenever I feel like you look, I always find a reason to celebrate. So—" She held up her glass. "Think and let's toast to it."

Matson shook his head. "I'd rather not."

"Okay, I'll go. Let's drink to . . . pain. The day we no longer feel it, only means we're dead." She giggled.

Matson couldn't help but smile. They clinked glasses.

"Amen," he seconded.

They drank. Rain curled her legs under her.

"So . . . you want to talk about what's on your mind?"

Matson hesitated, then looked at her.

"Yeah . . . tell me why, when I didn't know where else to go . . . I came here."

Rain was thrown by his honesty. She was all set to get in his cop head, using her body if she had to. But seeing the vulnerability in his eyes, she knew this wasn't cops and robbers. This was man and woman. Funny that it made her more comfortable . . .

"I don't know . . . do you think it's a good thing? I mean, because . . ." She let her voice trail off and looked at his ring.

He looked at it and chuckled bitterly. "It's just a ring. Nothing more . . . maybe less."

"Wow!" Rain replied and sipped her drink. "I . . . don't know what to say."

"No, it wasn't because of you . . . or rather, what we did . . ." Matson shook his head, downed his drink, embarrassed but blurted out, "I found out she did it, too."

Once he started, he couldn't stop. He had to get it out. If he didn't, he didn't know what he would do. Still, he couldn't remember his blackout, and that scared him.

Matson told her everything. Rain couldn't believe her ears. Love used to brag about how he was fucking the police, but she never knew what he meant because she knew Sonia wasn't a cop. Now she understood, and even though her mentality had always been, "Fuck the police!" She could see the pain in his eyes, hear it in his voice, and she knew he didn't deserve it. Sure, he had cheated on his wife, but she knew it had been a one-time thing. He was a good man, one that any good woman would appreciate.

Rain turned his face to hers gently.

"Listen, Tony, I'm not going to sugar coat this. But your so-called wife is a whore. This isn't about what she *did*; it's about who she *is*. And if you put up with that, it won't change her, it'll change *you*."

Matson nodded. He had already seen a sign of that. He covered his face.

"I—I don't know what to do."

Rain pulled her shirt over her head, unleashing the power of her beauty, but not to hurt . . . to heal.

"I do," she whispered.

She leaned him back and straddled his lap. Her body was already humming with the electricity of need. Since Jazmine had hit Kingfish and was taking over the streets, she had been neglecting Rain. She would come home too tired to talk and they barely had sex. Jazmine was feeling more like her roommate than her partner. She never imagined falling for a woman, but she had.

Hard.

She was loyal to Jazmine; she uprooted her life, risked her livelihood and went against family all for Jaz—

No, she had done those things for Swag before she even knew Jazmine existed.

Matson looked at her, taking in every inch. Just to look at her made his snake inflate under her throbbing pussy. They were two people left behind in different ways but had ended up in the same place

"You're beautiful," he whispered, running his hand over her plump breasts and pert nipples.

"You are, too," she replied.

When he flipped her over and laid her on the couch, covering her body with soft, tender kisses, she squirmed and loved each one. He licked her from her earlobes to her toes, making her cum without even penetrating her, until she begged, "Tony, I want you inside me please."

He cocked her left leg on top of the couch as he slid inside her fat, juicy pussy, her walls squeezing and massaging the length of his shaft with every stroke.

"Damn, you feel like heaven," he said.

"Ohhh, you're so deep," Rain sang, arching up to meet his thrusts.

She wrapped her legs around his back, urging him deeper. He licked and sucked her breasts while he long stroked her into a second orgasm, setting her pussy on fire and making her fiend to feel him cum.

"Please, daddy, cum in this pussy! Cum all in your pussy!" she cried.

He began to pound her when he felt the tension build in his stomach.

"Yes, daddy, yes, yes!"

"This pussy feels so good!"

"Cum in it!"

He pushed himself as deep as deep could be and released himself with jerks and grunts.

"Damn, Tony. Fuuuuuck," Rain ranted, her pussy still creaming.

He kissed her, tonguing her down, and when they looked at each other, they both had tears in their eyes.

-24-

"Gimme two," Swag grumbled, tossing out her dead cards.

The dealer slid her two more. She peeped. King of diamonds and a three of spades. Her poker face was perfect, but inside she was spazzing. She looked around at the five other players, all big ballers.

The place was an auto detailing shop by day, but a gambling spot by night. Bad bitches in heels and not much more, worked the room, bringing drinks and turning tricks when a lucky winner felt like celebrating with a piece of pussy. The smoke seemed to sit thick, never disappearing and hovering over the table.

"I'll raise you two-grand," a baller named Ramone said, tossing a wad into the pile.

The pot was already a groan over fifty-grand.

"I'll see that short shit and raise you five," spat a baller named Ace with a cocky chuckle, tossing another log on the fire.

Swag peeped her hand. A pair of nines, king high. She knew Ramone was bluffing. She had long ago read him, but Ace was impossible to read.

"I fold," she remarked, tossing her hand on the dead pile.

"Don't worry, baby," Derrick cooed, massaging her shoulders. "Your money losing. You want a drink?"

"Yeah," Swag replied, rubbing her hand over his hair.

Derrick switched away to get it.

"Faggot ass nigguh," a baller named Jerome grumbled.

Swag glanced at him. "You say somethin', fam'?"

Jerome looked at him but bit his tongue. "Naw."

Swag turned back to Ace as he raked in his winnings.

"So, what you think? I'm tellin' y'all, my number can't be beat."

"Yeah, but I fuck wit' Kingfish, playa'. Loyalty more important than a point or two," Ace replied.

The dealer dealt a new hand. Derrick brought Swag her drink and went back to massaging her shoulders.

"Yeah well. Fish retired." Swag chuckled, peeping her hand. It was straight bullshit.

"I need to hear that from Fish," Ace retorted.

Her losing streak was only adding to her frustration with the conversation.

"You hearin' it from *me*. I'm not givin' choices; it's either my number or zeros."

Jerome had heard enough. "Nigguh, fuck you 'posed to be? You think muhfuckas gonna let a goddamn homo thug run this—"

Boc! Boc! Boc! Boc! Boc!

Swag put five shots in his chest, firing the first sitting down, but like Samuel L. Jackson in *Menace II Society*, she stood up to finish the job. His body flipped out of the chair, so the last shot sparked off the concrete floor.

As soon as she set it off, Derrick pulled out twin .380s with pink pearl handles to hold her down.

Nobody moved. The sound of the shots rang in their stunned ears. Some of them were strapped, but Swag had made her move so swiftly, she had caught them all slipping.

"Anybody else got something slick to say, huh? I'm listenin'," Swag snarled, looking from face to face. "Now, as I was sayin' . . . Fish is officially retired. *I* retired him. So right now, I'm like God to y'all nigguhs. I make it *rain*! Any questions?"

She could see the heat in nigguhs' faces. They were heated, so she picked out one. Ace. She aimed her gun at him.

"Get down or lay down?"

Ace glared at her.

"Fuck you mean?"

"Just what I said!"

"Lay—"

Boc! Boc!

The two shots she sent through his face guaranteed a closed casket. His body slumped to the floor. She turned the gun on Ramone. He didn't even give her a chance to ask.

"Get down!" he blurted.

Swag smirked.

"Smart man . . . as for the rest of y'all, 'er body lay down! Fuck it, I'm turnin' this homicide into a robbery. I want all the money I lost up in here! Ramone, you good," she let him know.

Derrick went man to man relieving each man of his money, drugs, jewels, and gun. Everybody except Ramone.

"I got it all, daddy," Derrick snickered, holding up the bag.

"This right here I'ma call a down payment. Gimme a call and I'll front you consignment." Swag laughed. "555-3711."

With that, he and Derrick turned and walked out. They made their way to Derrick's red Porsche then pulled off.

"I'm glad you shot that motherfucka, daddy. He was startin' to get on my nerves," Derrick huffed as he turned the corner.

Swag was busy counting the money in the bag.

"I did it to make a point. Once these nigguhs think they can see me as a homo thug, then they'll always have something on their chest."

"Shit, you more man than any nigguh in there."

Swag chuckled. *If you only knew . . .*

"But, when you gonna give me some of this, *man*?" he purred, running his palm over the dildo between her legs.

Swag took his hand off and kissed it.

"I told you . . . my last relationship was hard on me. She broke my heart. I'm feelin' you like crazy, D, but I need to be sure about myself, you know?" Swag replied, running the 'I'm confused' game to perfection.

"I understand, baby. I like taking it slow," Derrick flirted.

"I just need to know I can trust you."

"You can."

"How I know that?" Swag countered, leading the conversation right where she wanted it.

He waited until they got to the light to reply, "How you need to know?"

"Miss Toni."

"Huh?"

She smirked.

"I don't trust him no more. How you feel about that?"

Without hesitation, he responded, "Baby, I'm ridin' with you."

Swag put her hand on the back of his neck and massaged it.

"He gotta go."

Derrick looked at her and replied, "Then he gone."

And just like that, Miss Toni's fate was sealed.

-25-

Kingfish had been around a lot of killers in his life, but none made him feel as uncomfortable as the albino with the coal black eyes. Especially with a name like Satan. Kingfish may've been a drug dealer, a killer, and fucked a few females younger than the law allowed, but he was a country boy at heart, so he considered himself a good Christian. Having a nigguh named Satan in his office seemed blasphemous. But business was business.

"I'm glad El Gordo sent you. I ain't gonna lie, this motherfucka Swag is a problem."

Satan smiled politely as one of Kingfish's waitresses, a shapely red-bone who looked like Solange Knowles, brought them drinks. She returned the smile and walked out.

"Believe me, Kingfish. I'm used to solving problems. I just need to know who this . . . Swag is."

"He hangs out with a faggot named Miss Toni. I don't know whose pitchin' or catchin', or if there's any playin' going on, period, but it is what it is. He also works for a detective named Coleman. Jazzy little bitch with a fly ass mouth. I don't know who's worse, him or her," Kingfish explained.

Satan's eyebrows went up.

"He works for the police? This I didn't know."

"Is that a problem?"

"No, but my fee just doubled," Satan replied, then sipped his drink.

"Man, I don't give a fuck! I just want these motherfuckas dead! I'll pay the cost."

"Music to my ears . . . I knew a Swag once and a—how did you put it—jazzy little bitch? Probably just a coincidence." He smirked.

The waitress walked back in.

"Kingfish, do you need anything else?"

"I do, if . . . you don't mind, Kingfish," Satan remarked.

"Naw, not at all."

Satan looked at the waitress.

"What's your name, sweetness?"

"Desiree."

"How would you like to make a thousand dollars?"

When he saw the greed leap in her eyes, he knew he had her . . .

########

They say the murderer always returns to the scene of the crime . . .

But seldom as a cop.

Jazmine stepped over the yellow crime scene tape stretched around the auto detailing shop she had been at hours earlier. She was there to investigate the double homicide she had committed.

"What've we got, officer?" Jazmine asked, detective badge swinging around her neck like a platinum chain and medallion.

"Oh. Hi, Detective. It's pretty ugly. The witness says that some guy named Swag murdered two people right over there."

"Witness?" she echoed; ears perked.

The officer looked around then and leaned toward her, speaking low. "We're keeping him on ice in the backroom. The guy's scared shitless!"

Jazmine kept her outer composure, but on the inside, she couldn't wait to see who the snitch was.

"Thanks."

She headed straight for the back and knocked on the door. Another officer stuck his head out.

"Oh, it's you, Detective. We've been waiting on you."

Jazmine walked in and recognized the face right away. He had been at the poker game sitting next to Ace. When she gave Ace the face-lift, some of the blood and brain matter splattered his face like tomato juice off a pizza.

"Detective Coleman." She extended her hand.

He shook it, or rather, he grabbed it with a shaking hand, and their hands vibrated momentarily. He looked like he had seen a shark attack.

"I'm Dolla."

"Your real name."

With a name like Horace, she understood why he had a nickname. She pulled up a chair and straddled it backward.

"Can you tell me what happened?" she requested, as if she didn't already know.

"Man . . ." he wrung his hands. "The shit was crazy! I never seen so much blood in my life . . . the kid Swag"

"Swag? Are you sure that's his name?"

He nodded.

"That's what I think Ace called him."

"But you're not sure!"

"I'm—almost positive, yo."

"But you just said you were sure."

Confusion planted; Dolla scratched his head. Jazmine looked at the officer and rolled her eyes like, Witnesses...

"Never mind the name. Can you describe him?"

"Yeah, yeah, he a light skin pretty boy with—"

Jazmine laughed.

"Pretty boy? You don't strike me as the . . . type," she signified.

He frowned. "Naw yo, *fuck* nah! I ain't no homo, yo. Hell no! It's just a figure of speech. He was just like . . . a light skin dude!"

Jazmine knew by questioning his manhood, she could scare him off a detailed description. Men are so easy . . .

"Listen . . . Horace. What you're giving up is kind of sketchy. I'm not doubting you, I just need . . . more," Jazmine urged, trying to pick his brain.

"More like what?"

Jazmine looked at the officer's name badge.

"Umm, Jones, could you get me a cup of coffee, black? Horace, you want one?"

He shook his head. "And make sure it's hot." She winked, letting him know she needed time alone.

Once the officer left, Jazmine scooted her chair closer to Dolla.

"Listen, between you and me, we've got a big investigation going on with this Swag, Swagga, whatever his name is. But he's got a lot of people on his team, even police, we think."

When he heard that, he looked at her, worry building like gathering clouds.

"The reason I'm telling you this is because you have to be careful who you talk to in the department. Now, besides the two officers, have you talked to anyone else?"

"Naw, naw, nobody. Yo ma, that dude is crazy! He can't find out about this, yo! I—I—I need witness protection or something!"

He already knows, she thought wickedly, but said, "Don't worry, Horace. You're safe with me," she said, giving him a smile that would've made a dying man believe in a brighter tomorrow.

He smiled back. "O–okay."

Jazmine sealed the deal by using her nail to scrape a drop of blood from his cheek, but she did it in such a way that had seduction whooping up his spine.

"Get this blood off your face, with your cute self. I think you and I are going to get along just fine, no?" she teased, pinning him with her hazel eyes.

Her hazel gaze had him flustered just as much as her green one had him petrified only hours earlier.

By the time Jones came back with the coffee, Dolla and Jazmine had already exchanged numbers and she was on her way out.

"Okay, Horace, I'll be in touch. Thanks, Jones," she said, taking the coffee from him.

She walked out with their eyes glued to her ass. As soon as she turned the corner, she dropped the coffee in a trash can and kept it moving.

As she drove away from the scene, for a second time, she thought about how she would use Dolla. Kill him? Eventually. After all, he was a snitch, so he couldn't be trusted. But in the meantime, having him around would give her another pawn to push.

Jazmine glanced in her rearview, just out of habit.

It paid off.

There were two of them in the car. Her every sense screamed at her. She made a quick left just to test them. A few seconds later, they turned the corner, too. She held her speed. She stopped at the light then made another left and a right. They did, too. They were far enough back to have fooled an amateur but too close to throw off a pro.

Jazmine gripped her stash gun instead of her service revolver, her mind whirling. *Who were they? Who sent them? Was it a hit or robbery?* She had basically made the whole city her enemy, so there was no way of finding out without making a scene in broad daylight.

When she got to the next light, she waited a moment, and then threw her siren bubble on top of her roof, then made a wide U-turn, siren whooping. Jazmine didn't look directly at them, she didn't have to, they were all too familiar.

Satan's goons.

Satan's colors. Jet black nigguhs with gold teeth. Her blood froze in her veins as she sped off, checking the rearview as if she were running on foot. The image of the tattoo on the dead girl's ass came back in 3D. There was no mistaking it. This was no coincidence. He had found her . . . just like she knew he would.

Jazmine went straight to the condo. When she arrived, she found Matson's car parked outside.

"Interesting . . ." she mumbled to herself.

She got out and started to go straight in, then stopped. She thought. Jazmine turned away and went around the side of the house. She wanted to see them as a fly on the wall, just to see if there was anything to unmask. What she saw only confirmed her assumption. She peeped in the window and saw Matson and Rain naked on the bed. But they weren't fucking. He was holding a folded newspaper and a pen, while Rain sat Indian style beside him, a bowl of ice cream between her legs, alternately feeding him and herself, spoonful's.

"Very interesting." She mumbled, heading back to the door. When she came into the bedroom, they both looked at her.

"Hey, baby," Rain sang.

Matson didn't speak. Just looked.

"Nobody said nothing about a party," Jazmine said matter-of-factly.

Matson and Rain exchanged a look, then Rain replied, "No party, baby."

"Rain, I need to talk to you," Jazmine remarked.

Matson got up and began to dress. When he walked past her, Jazmine said, "About the—"

He cut her off.

"She knew all about it."

"Meaning?" Jazmine probed.

"Ask Sonia," he spat, then walked out.

Once he left, Jazmine looked back at Rain.

"So, I see you got him back in the game?" Jazmine snickered. "Good, because we need him on the team. String him out. I need to know *everything* he does, and as soon as you can flip him completely, let me know," Jazmine explained.

Rain bit down on her bottom lip, pensively. Jazmine read her expression.

"What's wrong, Rain?"

"It's just . . . his wife."

"What about her?"

"I think it's fucked up how she played him, daddy. I mean, the game is the game, but goddamn . . . Tony's a good man and—"

"He's a cop, Rain. Don't forget that," Jazmine reminded her.

"So are you," Rain said, reminding *her*.

Jazmine smiled. But her eyes didn't.

"No, I'm not a cop. I'ma killer with a badge, a gangsta with a license . . . never forget *that*," she spat with a cold edge. "Now get dressed and get packed. We're moving."

"Moving? Why?"

"Because I said so," Jazmine snapped, vexed by Rain feeling sorry for Tony.

Rain put her hands on her hips. "Why you gotta be like that?"

"Why *you* gotta be on some bullshit? You think I give a fuck about his life, his wife, his missing daughter? Fuck no, I care about *me* and *mine*! So, you either with me or not. And Rain, I suggest you choose wisely," Jazmine warned.

"I'm always with you. I thought you knew."

"I thought I did, too. Now, pack."

"Okay, but at least tell me why."

Jazmine looked at her and said, ". . . He's here."

"Who?"

"The pastor."

Rain's eyes got big, because Jazmine had told her the story, so she knew shit was about to get ugly . . .

#########

"Ohh, Swag! I love you, baby!"

"I love you, too."

"Ri–Ri–Right there," Aria groaned, riding him hard, grinding his dick hard. He grabbed her hips and pulled her forcefully into every stroke.

"Oh fuck, daddy. My spottttt . . ." She melted.

He turned her over, pinning her legs over his shoulders, and stood up in the pussy, hitting bottom like he was trying to drill her through the mattress. She dug her nails in his neck, squeezing her pussy muscles at the same time, knowing exactly how to make him, "Aarggh!" He exploded inside her.

Relaxing in the glow, she rested her head on his chest.

"Why did you call me a thief?" she questioned, drawing imaginary circles on his chest.

He smiled into her hair, reliving the memory in his mind. "I didn't know you were so beautiful . . . but the minute I looked at you, you stole my heart."

Her heart skipped a beat as she smiled to herself.

"So, are you?" he asked.

"Am I what?"

"Going to give it back?"

She bit his nipple playfully. "Never," she vowed.

With each day, the two of them grew closer and more alike. The time between heaven and hell wasn't long, not even thirty days until Satan came for her, but that's what makes time precious, brevity.

He taught. He molded her. She already knew how to handle a gun, but Swag taught her to master it.

Boc! Boosh! Boc! Boosh! Boc! Boosh! Boc! Boosh!

Swag tossed coke bottles up in the air, and she picked them off making the glass shatter with the .45 she had come to love. He taught her how to ride a motorcycle. He started her out on a YZ motor bike then worked her up to a Kawasaki Goo, then a 700, increasing the difficulty until he finally let her push his Ninja 1200. It sat so wide and thick under her; she could only touch the ground on her tippy toes. He got on behind her.

"Can you handle this?" Swag needed to be sure.

Aria looked him up and down, over her left shoulders. "I can handle anything you got."

He laughed. She revved the bike to red line.

"Try anything and I'll kill us both," she said playfully, using his line from the night of the kidnapping, then zoomed off.

They only spoke Creole and French, to the point she began to dream in those languages.

"Why don't you speak in English?" she asked.

"It doesn't make sense."

Everything seemed to get better, except her relationship with the old woman. She still refused to speak to Aria, although, Aria would sometimes feel the old woman staring at her. When she looked, the old woman wouldn't look away, but neither would Aria. What she saw in the old woman's eyes wasn't hate or resentment, it was pity. Two days later, she found out why.

Aria pretended to be sleep, but something told her the old woman knew she was faking, but she wanted her to hear.

"A storm's comin'," she said as she sat gently rocking in her chair.

"I can smell it," Swag replied.

The old woman nodded.

"I 'tend on movin' on from here. Leavin' tomorrow . . . you comin?" she asked, looking at him directly.

He knew exactly what she was asking. "I'm not leaving her, Nana," Swag replied firmly.

"He say he comin' for her. Wants me to leave it 'tween you two."

"He'll get what he comin' for then," he gritted.

"He still your father," she shot back forcefully. "Don't forget it."

Swag bit his tongue.

"That one there . . . her hollow inside, nothin' but pain and anger. Her soul is dead. Is that what you see?"

"You the one with the eyes, Nana."

"Have they ever been wrong?" she shot back pointedly.

He couldn't say anything, because they hadn't.

"She gonna cost you your life. You know that, don't you?"

Without hesitation, Swag answered, "We all gotta die of something. I guess love's a good enough reason as any."

"Love makes a man do foolish things."

"What would you do, Nana?" he asked, knowing the answer because he knew her story.

She grunted inaudibly, then used her staff to help herself get up.

"Be leavin' in the mornin' fo' first light," she said, then walked out.

##########

When he got in the bed, Aria's face was full of tears.

"I—I don't want you to die, Swag. Please, I—I'll go back to him."

He kissed her gently. "That would kill me, too."

He held her tight, feeling her body vibrate with tears.

"Why did she say I'm hollow, baby? I'm not hollow, I'm not empty!"

"Shh, I know," he replied, his voice as comforting as a blanket. But deep down knowing, the old woman had never been wrong . . .

The next morning, Swag watched the old woman float off down the swampy river, her long white dreads draped down her back. She stood in the small wooden boat, using a long pole to propel her forward. She never looked back, and once she disappeared into the moonlight of the false dawn, he knew he would never see her again.

A few hours later, the rains began. They got heavier and the winds blew harder, swirling. Swag knew this wouldn't be just another storm.

And then he came.

"Swag . . . this doesn't have to be like this," Satan called out, outside of the house. "Send her out and I'll let you go."

Swag peeked out the window. They had the house surrounded. They seemed to come out of nowhere.

Creeping in under the cover of the storm. Satan was back in Vietnam. His whole squadron armed to the teeth.

Aria took one look and damn near fainted.

"Baby, please, let me go! You can't win!"

Swag cracked a crooked grin and replied, "Neither can they."

He threw open the closet and pulled a heavy book bag and tossed it to her. The weight almost knocked her down. He then grabbed an AK-47 and several banana clips.

"Come on!" he barked.

He led her into the back room, and he opened up a trap door in the floor that opened up to the bare ground beneath the house. As soon as they both went through, Satan's team began to swiss cheese the house after making his announcement. Satan waited a moment, then receiving no reply, gave the nod.

The goons let the .50 caliber weapons rip. The bullets seemed to be rocking the house on its foundation. Chunks of wood flew everywhere, opening up holes that were big enough for a man to crawl through.

Aria kept her head down on Swag's chest as they lay safely underneath the barrage. He slipped the clip in the AK-47 and looked at every angle. All he could see were legs all around the house, but on one side, there were fewer pair. He chose that as his escape route. He took the .47 off his pants and handed it to Aria.

"You ready?" he asked.

She took a deep breath, then nodded.

"It's just like busting bottles." He winked.

They belly crept to the edge of the house. As soon as the crew went back to reload, Swag let loose a swarm of his own.

Bbbbbbbbrrrrrpppppppppp!

The bullets buzzed and bit into flesh like angry African bees with full metal jackets. Bodies started falling as hard as the rain.

"Let's go!" he bellowed. Then he grabbed the book bag, and they took off running.

As soon as Satan heard the different caliber blast, he yelled, "Go! They are around the back!"

By the time the goons made it around, Swag and Aria had disappeared into the swampy forest. The goons blasted anyway, hitting nothing but the tree trunks and leaves.

The wind whipped harder, knocking one man off his feet, but Satan stood firm.

"Fuck are you waiting for?"

They took off after them.

Swag knew the area like the back of his hand, so even in the blinding storm, he knew his way. He had purposely gone one way, then cut back almost ninety degrees until he had doubled back on them.

"Wait, baby. I have to catch my breath," Aria complained.

"Get on my back if you're weak," he teased with a straight face. She pushed him and kept going. Her lungs burned, but she was determined to be strong.

They came out on a dirt path. Underneath a car cover was his old pickup truck. He opened the door, checked for the keys in the ignition, then turned to Aria.

"Go. Drive straight to New Orleans. Whatever they're using as the biggest shelter, I'll meet you there," he instructed her.

"No, Swag. I'm not going without you!" she sassed back, pouting.

With the swiftness of a striking cobra, he grabbed her around the throat and hissed, "Don't ever tell me what you won't do! Now go! I love you!" He kissed her hard and long, the sensation of the kiss and the grip of his hand combining into a swoon in her head. He let her go.

"I–I love you, too!"

He handed her the book bag and she got in under the wheel. Once she had driven off, he went to the job at hand.

##########

Satan was livid that they had gotten away. He was so mad, that when one of his goons said, "Boss, the storm! We have to go!"

Boc!

He gave him a bullet between the eyes that made him look like a red dot Indian. He collapsed to the ground.

"Anybody else want to go?" he yelled out.

No one said a word.

Swag worked his way back around Satan's squad. Once he was in position, he began picking them off almost at will. The confusion the storm created, along with the fact that he was at home and they weren't, had them spooked. They were shooting each other by mistake.

Satan stood in the clearing, hearing the muffled sounds of automatic fire under the whip of the wind. From the cries of anguish and pain, he could count backward, knowing his team was being picked apart.

Unable to take it anymore, he snatched up a .50 Cal from one of the dead bodies and went off into the bush.

"I should've come by my goddamn self!" he mumbled, gun trained and ready like a true vet.

But it had been decades since he'd been in combat, and even though it was all still fresh in his mind, Swag had one more advantage.

He was in constant combat in the here and now.

Satan followed the smell of the gunfire and blood, the gusts carrying it upwind right to him. The winds made him brace himself against a tree. He spotted the river and headed toward it. The rain cut down on his visibility. He tried to stay sharp.

Swag was sharper.

The force of the river's current carried Swag right up on Satan and concealed his scent. When he came out of the water, he took Satan totally by surprise.

"Put it down," Swag grumbled.

Satan smiled.

"I taught you well, I see. The irony speaks for itself," he replied, dropping the gun, putting his hands up and turning to Swag. "Where is she?"

"Safe."

"I see . . . you sent her to New Orleans."

"And I'm sending you to hell," Swag seethed, took aim and . . .

Saw the face of his Nana.

"He's still your father . . ."

Swag knew she was connected to both of them. To pull the trigger would be to kill her, too. Satan saw the hesitation.

"What are you waiting for? Shoot." Satan smirked.

Swag fought with himself. With his only weakness. The fact that his love was stronger than his hate.

"Leave her out of it. This is between you and me," Swag remarked.

Satan knew what he was saying. He was willing to spare Satan and jeopardize retaliation in exchange for Aria's life.

"She is what's between you and me," Satan replied.

"Let her go and I'll let you go. Isn't that what you offered me?" Swag sneered.

Satan smiled.

"I'll find you. You know that, don't you?"

"Probably."

"And when I do, I won't be merciful."

Swag's trigger finger itched. "I'll let you break Nana's heart then. Not me," he replied.

Satan would always remember his mother with tenderness, but he didn't have Swag's weakness. His hate was stronger.

"Okay."

Swag waved the gun. "Then walk away. Before I change my mind."

Satan turned slowly, bracing against the wind. "You should've killed me, son." He laughed, but when he turned to look, Swag was already gone.

-26-

"Detective Coleman," the male detective said, sticking his head in her office.

"Yes?"

"I've got a guy out here that says he knows the guy that committed the double homicide at the gambling joint."

Jazmine perked up.

"Another witness?"

He shrugged. "He wouldn't say."

"Okay . . . send him in," she replied.

She prepared herself to run her usual flim-flam, not knowing the flim-flam was about to be on her.

"Detective . . . Coleman?"

She didn't even have to look up to know who it was. It was inevitable. After the dead girl's tattoo and the goons on her tail, she knew the day would come when she'd hear that voice again.

She looked up into his cold smile. Her first instinct was to pull her gun. He read the twitch.

"Is there something wrong, Detective Coleman?" Satan inquired, his expression and tone toying with her. "You seem . . . tense."

Her heart beat like a thousand stampeding horses, half out of fear, half out of fury.

"You choose to do this here? You think this place makes you safe?" she challenged.

"I could ask you the same thing . . . but forgive me if I seem confused. You are Detective Coleman, aren't you?"

"Yes," she gritted, holding her composure.

He nodded.

"Because you look like someone I once knew well. Extremely well. It's almost like . . . de ja vu." He smirked; his cold black gaze fixated on her every breath.

"Get to the point."

Satan leaned toward her desk.

"*You* are the point, my dear. You have always been the point . . . but I'm getting ahead of myself. I'm here to share what I know of the murders," he remarked, sitting back and crossing his legs casually.

Jazmine eyed him hard.

"You know, I could say you were a maniac . . . some kind of a nut case. I could say I thought you were armed and so I fired once . . . wildly. It wasn't my fault that the bullet blew your fuckin' brains out. Lucky shot," she hissed, her hand itching to grab her automatic from her holster.

He smiled but disregarded her provocation.

"You see, Detective, this Swag was once a killer in New Orleans. I've been tracking him . . . and her since Katrina. You can say I lost them in the storm. But I found them in Mississippi, but they slipped by me. Once they got to Alabama, it got easier because they left a trail of blood any man could've followed. A regular Bonnie and Clyde, these two." He chuckled. "I almost caught up with them in Atlanta. Room 203 at the Hyatt . . . Then they came here. But I knew they would because, well . . . I'm getting ahead of myself. My point being, these last two murders were nothing."

As he charted her and Swag's every move, Jazmine's stomach knotted like a pretzel. Room 203 . . . that had been their room. If he knew that, she knew he had been close the whole time.

"You aren't half the man he was," she spat spitefully, hoping, *praying*, he'd make a move, trying to provoke him so she could end it all right there.

Satan laughed in her face, seeing what she was trying to do.

"Sticks and stones, Aria. I mean—" He winked. "Detective Coleman. As for being half the man, you've been with enough to be an expert? Foom!" he spat, calling her a whore in Creole as he stood.

Jasmine's jaw clenched. She laid her gun on the table, finger 'pon cock.

"Say it again," she seethed.

He smiled down at her. "I'll be in touch."

"Where can you be reached?"

"I can't . . . but you can." He winked, then walked out.

When Satan left, Jazmine had to close the blinds on her door so no one would see her crying. Her tears came from relief, shame, frustration, and anger, but the angry tears burned the hottest.

<h1 style="text-align:center">-27-</h1>

"Who is it?"

"Regina," came the gum-popping reply.

The petite, La-La Anthony looking chick peeked out the peephole and saw the cute little cinnamon number staring back at her. She didn't know the girl, but she knew Kingfish liked a house full of pussy. So, thinking, the more the merrier, she opened the door.

"Where's Kingfish?"

"In the back," La-La answered, locking the door.

Ffffffffffzzzztt!

It happened so fast La-La didn't know her throat was cut. It stung, but the worst part was the choking. She couldn't scream.

"Shhhh," Jazmine sang, "it'll be over in a minute."

La-La slid down the door, pop eyes bulging, holding her throat. No one heard because the Lil Wayne song blaring in the living room drowned out everything. When Jazmine emerged from the hallway into the living room, she found two females smoking kush on the couch.

Whhhhwwww! Whhhhwwww!

Two silenced shots. Two exploding heads, the wall blood stained, and the blunt left burning in the lap of a dead person.

Jazmine continued on her mission. In the bedroom, Kingfish was lying back like a beached whale while a butt naked bitch with a stripper's body sucked his tadpole.

As soon as she walked in, his eyes opened and focus on her. "You!" he barked.

Jazmine raised the gun and blew the back of the girl's head all over his chest. Her reflexes made her jaw clench, almost biting his dick off.

"Eeeeeeeeeeeeee!" he bellowed like a sounding like a mule, trying to unclench her dead jaw.

Jazmine tucked the gun and extracted a six-inch blade from her waist. As soon as she got upon him, as she stuck the knife in his windpipe slow, she said in Swag's voice, "Guess who, you fat bastard!"

In his last excruciating minutes, he wrapped his mind around the face he was seeing and the voice he was hearing. His eyes registered recognition.

"Y-y-you?"

Jazmine smiled. In the background she heard a toilet flush.

"You sent Satan at me, so now I'm sending you to see him. Fair exchange," she replied, then rammed the knife up to the hilt into his throat. His body jerked and flopped, then lay still while dark red blood ran out of his mouth. That told her he was dead.

In the background, Jazmine heard the pitter patter of galloping feet.

"Shit!" she cursed, turning and running out the door.

She saw the girl as she ran out of the apartment. She aimed and fired but a second too late. Her gun was empty. She reloaded as she hurried out of the apartment.

The girl was just getting to the open elevator. Jazmine aimed and blew a hole in her back, trying to blow out her heart.

"Oh God!" the girl gasped, stumbling into the elevator.

The doors were closing, Jazmine aimed and fired, and the shot split the girl's dome, making the elevator look like someone spilled tomato soup all in it. The door whooshed closed.

"Shoulda took the stairs," Jazmine laughed as she did just that.

-28-

Derrick told Miss Toni to meet him at the storage unit where Miss Toni and Swag had all the coke.

"Where's Swag?" Miss Toni asked when Derrick arrived with some other dude.

"He said he had to handle something. He said just give me twenty of them things," Derrick requested.

Miss Toni and Milly stepped out of the car. The whole situation felt like an ill-sized stiletto to Miss Toni. Shit just didn't fit. He knew Derrick, knew how grimy he could get, so in the back of his mind, he wondered why Swag would send him in her place.

It didn't take long to find out.

Click clack!

Derrick snatched the gun from his waist and threw it in Miss Toni's face. "Sorry, sweetheart, but it's time for a change in the organization," Derrick snickered snidely.

The other dude had Milly covered. Miss Toni raised his hands.

"So, you robbin' us? How you think Swag gonna take that?" Miss Toni asked.

Derrick chuckled wildly. "Take it? My baby sent me! So *we're* robbin' *you*!"

Miss Toni had figured that was the case, but he knew he could pick Derrick's brain in a couple of ways. One...

"Can I at least know why mother deserves so treacherous a treatment?"

Derrick stepped up close, basking in the moment. He truly believed Swag was fucking Miss Toni. So, he felt like the next girl stunting on the ex-girl.

"Daddy don't trust your triflin' ass no more. Can't say I blame him, since he got himself a *real* bitch, now," Derrick boasted.

"Is that right?" Miss Toni smirked.

"Damn right!"

He had heard enough and . . .

Boc! Boc! Boc! Boc!

Now Miss Toni was picking Derrick's brain, literally, picking it off his clothes after Lilly dropped him and his partner hot. Derrick had noticed he only saw one of the twins. You *never* just saw one of the twins. He thought about it, but he was too intent on doing what *Daddy* told him . . .

The bullets had struck him in the neck and face, knocking him up against the side of the storage. Miss Toni pulled out his own gun and stood over him.

"Bitch, you still dead! Daddy gonna flip when he finds out!" Derrick groaned, the chill of death slowly climbing his spine.

Miss Toni laughed. "You stupid, misguided motherfucka! You wanted some dick so bad, you fell for a rubber one!"

Derrick frowned and coughed up blood. "Wh–what?"

"Dumb ass nigguh! Yo' daddy is a bitch . . . literally!" Miss Toni laughed, then put two in his brain and left him limp.

He turned to Milly. "Get the coke and let's get the hell out of here."

Before they could move, they heard . . .

"Freeze!"

"Don't move!"

Click-Clack! Click-Clack!

"Drop it!"

The sound of boots and cocking weapons filled their ears. Even Lilly who lay on the roof of the opposite storage unit was pinned down. The black jacketed

SWAT team seemed to explode out of nowhere, then swarmed everywhere. It had to be at least twenty of them. Miss Toni knew it was futile to try and resist.

He expected Jazmine to come walking up. Since she couldn't get him as him, he felt her back up plan was to get him as her. It would be just like Jazmine.

But she wasn't the one who approached him. Miss Toni had never seen the albino officer before, and he prided himself on knowing most, if not all the cops. But this face was new.

"Cuff 'em," the albino ordered.

They snatched Lilly off the storage unit and cuffed her while slamming Miss Toni and Milly against the car, cuffing them.

"You ain't Metro," Miss Toni concluded. "Who you? FBI? DEA?

The albino smiled.

"Worse. H-E-L-L." He chuckled, and then Miss Toni and the twins went black as the chemicals from the handkerchief put them to sleep . . .

-29-

"Daddy!" Felecity yelled happily as soon as she came in the house. Matson was sitting on the couch. Waiting. She wrapped her little arms around his neck, and instinctively he hugged her, falling into the daddy-daughter moment until he realized . . .

It *wasn't* a daddy-daughter moment.

He broke the hug. Sonia saw the flinch and said, "Felecity . . . honey, go up to your room. Let mommy and daddy talk."

"Okay," she sang, then skipped up the stairs.

Once her absence set in, Sonia asked, "Have . . . have you heard anything about Bianca?"

Matson rubbed his head, shaking it slowly.

"Nothing. We've got the best in the department on it. We're even co-coordinating with the FBI. Most abductors leave some kind of trail. These didn't . . . the FBI thinks it may be . . . human traffickers."

Sonia's voice caught in her throat, and she covered her mouth with one hand and her stomach with the other. Her sobs made her knees weak. Matson stood up and hugged her. She clung to him for dear life. He wanted to cling to her . . . dear God. He wanted to cling to her, but he . . . just . . . couldn't. His hug remained comforting but distant.

Feeling the vibe, Sonia pulled back.

"I-I'm okay." She sniffed as she sat down.

Matson sat beside her, handing her the box of Kleenex off the coffee table.

"Th—thank you."

"Yeah."

Silence . . . cold silence . . . uncomfortable silence . . . painful silence . . .

"How . . . how are you?" Sonia asked, ignoring the fact that she had smelled a slight whiff of another woman's perfume on him.

"I don't know," he answered truthfully. "I've been all day thinking . . . and all-night wandering. Our love changing and still has me in a fog."

Sonia seized his hand and looked into his eyes.

"Love *hasn't* changed, baby. Tony, I'm so sorry you had to find out this way, but I am even more sorry for what I did. I—I was a fool; I did you so wrong. I know that you and I alone can't fix this. Do you want to fix it, Tony?"

Looking in her eyes, he found it hard to say what he knew he should.

"Yes."

She breathed a relieved breath and squeezed his hand.

"I do too. I love you. Our family has been through so much. We need to go to God; we need to give it to God. Will you go to church with me? Tomorrow's Sunday. I know we haven't been in a while, but I think it's time. Jesus will give us our little girl back and the strength back in our union."

Hearing her words, she sounded so sure about the solution. And because he felt so helpless, so utterly lost, what she said made total sense.

He looked into her eyes, mustered a smile and replied, "Yes, Sonia, I'll go to church with you."

She returned his smile, and her tears shone like diamonds in her eyes.

"Thank you, baby. I love you so much." She hugged him and he hugged her tight. It felt good to her, but in the back of her mind, she couldn't help but wonder, whose perfume did she smell?

##########

It had been so long since he'd attended church, Matson forgot how comforting and uplifting it could be. The sounds of the choir, all singing in one voice, unified, soulful, each song a prayer of itself. He walked in carrying Felecity and holding Sonia's hand. All smiles. The people in the pews smiled back. The perfect family.

If they only knew . . .

Once the choir had uplifted the spirits, the reverend stepped to the pulpit to feed their souls.

"Yesssss, brothers and sisters, gawd is *truly* our strength in the storm," the reverend began.

"Yes, Jesus!" someone shouted.

"Because, when weeee can't, he can!"

"Yes, he can!"

"Preach!"

The reverend pranced the stage like a peacock out of place.

"You see, brothers and sisters, as Jesus says in . . ."

Matson sat absorbing every word, taking in the wisdom and whispering his own, "Amen," until the preacher said, "Because Gawwwwddd puts no burden on you greater than you can bear."

His eyes popped open for reasons he didn't understand at the time, and his mind went back to the sight of Rain's naked, voluptuous body, back arched on the bed, while he watched her through the window. He had never done anything like that before. He was a man who prided himself on doing the right thing. He had made mistakes, but he was always man enough to admit them. But he knew he was a good man, a good husband, a good cop.

But he was still a man . . .

And in that moment at that window, he had been so bent on doing the right thing—catching Jazmine. He ended up doing something he didn't expect . . . catching himself. It was in that moment he felt all his problems had begun, in that moment that he slipped, it had unraveled like a loose thread, until his life had become a useless ball of yarn. He felt like a first-time offending shoplifter who the judge sentenced to *life*. He felt no forgiveness, no grace, no divine love, so when he heard the preacher say, "Because Gawwwddd puts no burden on you greater than you can bear," the sheer absurdity of the statement made him snicker, and that soon became a chuckle, that became laughter, loud laughter, the kind postal workers probably cackle right before they . . .

"Stop, Rev, stop! Are you kidding me? Are you fucking kidding me?" Matson laughed.

The whole congregation collectively gasped, hearing the curse. It sounded like a communal inhale.

"Baby, let's go," Sonia whispered, feeling a thousand eyes all over her. She had seen that look in his eyes before. It didn't end well. Matson ignored her.

"Why are you *lying* to these people, Rev? No burden greater than you can bear? Really? Do you believe that?"

"Yes . . . yes I do, brother. Please don't—" the reverend answered nervously, until Matson stood and cut him off.

"You think God *loves* us? You call what you see in the world *love*? Either he's too weak to stop it, or he's enjoying the fucking show!"

Two ushers approached.

"Oh brother, we're going to—"

"What?" Matson spat, pulling his gun. "You're going to what?"

The two ushers jumped back, the congregation screamed and started to flee, but Matson waved his gun.

"Sit down! Everybody sit *down*! You want to know the truth, don't you? Ain't that what you came for? Huh? Is it? The truth is, you've been lied to! Bamboozled! Hood winked!" He cackled. "God ain't a ruler, he's a *ruler*, a wooden elementary school ruler, measuring every *inch* of your lives and the minute, the *second* you fall short, he'll destroy you! A man could walk the straight and narrow his whole life, but if he stumbles, look out! You wake up and realize you're married to a whore, and you don't even know who *you* are! That's your fucking Gawwwddd! Wake up . . . you live, you die, and in between, you fucking suffer!" Matson ranted.

Sonia sat cradling Felecity, both crying their eyes out.

"Daddy, please!" Felecity sobbed.

"You see? The baby doesn't even know who I am . . . Ask your mother who your goddamn daddy is," he seethed, then looked at Sonia with disgust, hate, and contempt, and said, "I want a divorce."

Then he calmly put his gun back in his holster and walked out of the church.

-30-

Jazmine watched as the black dildo strap on slid in and out of Rain's wet pussy. She spread Rain's ass cheeks wider and pumped the dildo in and out in a furious pace.

"Ohh, daddy, right there, right there!" Rain cried out.

But Jazmine was in a zone, her mind racing, a thousand miles away. All her anger and frustration were the only things present as she punished Rain, thrust after thrust after thrust.

"Ja–Ja–Jaz, wait, baby. Please stop," Rain pleaded, after having cum twice and her pussy feeling raw from the burn of the plastic, it damn near had her pussy smelling like a get-away on Pirelli tires.

"Jazmine!" she barked, bucking Jazmine off her.

"I thought you liked it rough," Jazmine answered snidely, lying back against the headboard.

Rain looked at her, trying to read her expression.

"What's wrong with you?"

Everything, Jazmine thought bitterly.

Her mind was on the crime scene at the storage unit. Seeing Derrick face down, damn near headless, and the empty storage unit told her all she needed to know.

"I should've handled it myself," she had mumbled to herself, standing over Derrick's fly-infested body.

Now she had Miss Toni as an enemy, and he knew her secret. Knew she was both her and him to the world. Jazmine shuddered to think how he'd use this information. Then on top of that, the faggot had all the coke! Jazmine had only seen less than eight hundred thousand so far. She had made a move to take it all and ended up with nothing. She had underestimated Miss Toni, and he had beaten her. She hated being beaten.

"Fuck!" she blurted, hitting the back of her head against the headboard, like: Stupid, stupid, stupid . . .

"So, we're back to that, huh? You're not gonna tell me what's goin' on?" Rain asked.

Jazmine just shook her head and looked around the tiny bedroom. The apartment she chose was in the cut, but it felt like a shoebox.

"Shit . . . just fucked up, Rain. Okay? I fucked up and overplayed my hand," Jazmine admitted.

"Meaning?" Rain probed.

"Miss Toni got the coke," Jazmine replied.

Rain's eyes bulged. "All of it?"

Jazmine could only nod, yanking off the strap and hurling it at the wall.

"So . . . what about the Cartel? Once they get at Kingfish—" Rain began, but Jazmine cut her off.

"*I* got at Kingfish," she spat, so disgusted with herself, she didn't know what to do but pace. "I fuckin' killed the fall guy *and* I missed Miss Toni! I overplayed my hand!"

Rain shook her head. "So, what are we gonna do?"

"Get it back . . . somehow."

"And if we don't?"

Jazmine chuckled.

"Then El Gordo will send a team through here to lay shit down and ain't no tellin' if Fish told him who robbed him!" she reasoned, knowing deep down he did, which is what led Satan right to her doorstep.

"Then we should go. Just . . . leave," Rain suggested.

"And go where? El Gordo runs the whole coast! And the pastor . . ." She shook her head and looked out the window at the falling rain.

She wished Swag was here. With him, she knew she'd survive. Now, she felt like iron was over her head and she was drowning fast. Jazmine listened to the rain and watched it gather in puddles all along the curb. She wished it would rain harder, hard like the rain that had washed away her former life . . .

##########

The levees broke . . .

Aria saw the results with her own eyes. The truck had stalled and refused to budge.

"No, no, no, please go," she prayed desperately, but to no avail.

And then she felt the rumble. Like the rumbles of a hungry stomach, like the earth itself needed to be fed, replenished, and sated. Then she saw it in the rearview. The rushing water looked like a puff of unraveling smoke in the distance, but as it came closer, it looked like a ball of wild bulls from Spain, running along the street, running along the walls of the city, swallowing everything as it barreled down on her.

"Oh. My. God!" She gasped.

Aria quickly rolled up her windows and put the book bag on her back. She knew if she got out, she'd be drowned in the powerful current. Her only chance was hoping the angry wave buoyed the trunk and turned it into a boat that would float her to safety. It didn't . . .

Whoooooosh!

The force of the water hit the rear of the truck, like one of the bulls had lowered its horns and flung the rear ass up. The rest of the waves did the rest, carrying the truck forward as if standing on its head, throwing Aria up against the windshield with enough force to crack it.

She screamed. The sound filled the truck but was muffled by the angry roar of nature unleashed. The second rush turned the truck on its roof, pinning Aria to the ceiling as she floated down the street. She was completely submerged, the window groaning and trembling with the weight of the water trying to get in to consume her. Some seeped in and trickled down the window, running like hungry jaws, watering at the mouth.

The world flowed by, upside down and under water, a modern-day Atlantis. She heard a solid thump on the passenger window glass. She looked.

"Noooooooo!" she bellowed, covering and scurrying to the other side of the truck.

It was a human face . . . eyes wide open, glassy, seeing nothing because it was a face of death, a look of horror etched on it, a telltale sign that it had died in fear. Its shirt got caught on the mirror, so it clung on, looking at Aria, warning her of her fate if she slipped.

Having swallowed the truck whole, the wave gurgled on, satisfied, its angry head leaving her in the peaceful wake of its stream. She knew it was time to get out. She rolled down the window, allowing the anxious rush of water to pour in. Within seconds the truck was flooded.

As soon as it was, Aria pulled herself through the window and swam out. A moment later she exploded through the surface and back into the down pouring rain.

The under guts of the truck floated along on top of the water, so she climbed on top of it, resting on the transmission to catch her breath. She looked down and saw the body stuck to the mirror. She reached down and untwisted the shirt, setting the body free to float along as it streamed away, she watched the body bob face down, until something of great force snatched it under. She shuddered to think what it was.

All around her, her city was underwater. It was like the skies had opened up, and God was finally going to punish the city for its sin like a modern-day Sodom and Gomorrah. Aria spotted a house. It sat up a little higher than the street, so only its first floor was half drowned. She decided to try and get to the house and hopefully find help or at least refuge on its upper floor. She readied herself to dive back into the water, looking around, hoping whatever had pulled the body under wasn't still around. Just in case, she pulled one of the guns out of the book bag, kissed it, said a quick prayer, and dove in.

Splash!

The water was cold and murky, the current stronger than she anticipated. It snatched the gun easily, as if her hand had been greased with butter. She had to fight hard to swim sideways against the current, but she finally reached the house. She grabbed the corner porch and pulled herself out of the water.

Aria scrambled to her feet and climbed the porch. The water had already reached the top of the porch, knee deep.

"Hello! Hello! Anybody here? Hey!" she called out, banging on the door with heavy hands.

No one responded. The strength of the storm wasn't only in the water; the winds were just as powerful. A strong gust blew across her so hard, had she been five pounds lighter, it would've blown her clean off the porch. Without hesitation, she smashed the porch window with the book bag, swinging its weight like a bat.

Kkkkkssssssh! Went the window.

She knocked out the jagged edges and carefully climbed through.

"Hello!" she called out again, while at the same time pulling another gun from the book bag.

The house was silent and stale. The smell of a place whose door hadn't been open in days. She ran to the phone and checked for a tone, but it was dead. She heard a crash on the porch. She looked out the window; the water was already lapping at the windowsill. The water was rising like the whole city was a tub. She had to get upstairs.

Aria ran for the stairs, then stopped and ran into the kitchen. She snatched opened the refrigerator, only to find that someone had already beaten her to the stripping. The only thing inside was a milk gallon jug filled with water and a couple of squishy tomatoes. She snatched them up, then she rambled through the cabinets. When she found corn starch and a couple of cans of pork and beans, she laughed like she had pulled the lever on a slot machine and it came up all cherries.

"Yes!"

She heard the water pouring through the window, so she quickly gathered up her winnings, found a can opener, tossed it all in the book bag, then headed up the stairs.

Within an hour, the water was halfway up the stairs, the rain was still falling unabatedly, and the wind was still howling.

At that rate, the second floor would be flooded by nightfall. The only higher ground was the roof, but after that, if the water kept rising . . .

Aria wondered if she had made the wrong decision. If she should've stayed on the floating truck. She shook it off. No need to dwell on it. She waited until the water had poured around her ankles before she decided she couldn't wait any longer, and climbed on the roof, tossing the book bag and several blankets out before she went.

Once she reached the roof, she ripped slits in each of the blankets and wore them, all six, like ponchos. The rain would soak the top two quickly, but she hoped by the time she reached the sixth and final blanket, the rain would've stopped.

It didn't.

The sun began to go down and the rain still beat upon her mind, body, and soul. The roof she was on was a gable styled roof, slanted at a forty-five-degree angle and shingled, with a chimney. The water rose until only the tip and not much else stayed above the water. If she stretched her legs out fully, her ankles would be under water. While she sat there watching the water rise, wondering when . . . if it would stop, she thought about if it didn't. She wondered would she rather drown, or just take one of the guns and blow her own brains out. Even after the rain stopped, the water continued to rise, and then it began to slow down and then . . . stopped.

"Thank you," she whispered fervently.

The night was pitch black. Once her eyes adjusted, she could see the soft shimmer of the water in the moonless night. Somewhere, something plunked in the water. She kept her eyes peeled, her back against the chimney, a .45 in both hands.

"Swag, baby, please be okay," she whispered in Creole, holding back the tears because she knew this was no time for them.

The sun rose without her catching a wink and she saw her city . . .

Or what was left of it. Everywhere she looked, all she could see was water. The whole city had virtually disappeared except for the peak of roof tops and church steeples. She felt like she had been washed out to sea.

Aria saw a gator gliding swiftly toward her. She quickly stood up on the tippy point of the roof and held both guns as tight as a grudge.

The gator, eyes just above the water, eyeing her as it glided by, seemed to say, "Naw . . . you too strong right now. I'll see you in a couple of days."

"Play with me if you want to! I'll die wearin' a brand-new pair of gator boots!" she shouted, watching the tail leave an S-shaped trail in the water.

Her stomach growled. She cranked open a can of beans, wishing she had thought to grab a spoon. The taste of the pork and beans sparked a memory. She was a little girl back in Shreveport, Louisiana. She used to love beans and franks. That was before . . .

"Baby, baby, don't do that, you'll wrinkle your dress," Miranda nagged with a motherly whine in her voice.

"Okay, Mommy. I like my dress. It's pretty," an eight-year-old Aria chimed, twirling in her brand-new yellow dress and patent leather shoes.

Miranda smiled and pinched her cheek. "But not as pretty as you. Now, be very good, because a nice man's coming to see us today."

"Who? My daddy?" Aria questioned with breathless anticipation.

She had always dreamed one day her daddy would come back.

Miranda didn't respond.

Aria's eyes got wide, thinking she knew why.

"You're getting married?"

A strange look passed over Miranda's face, but she blinked it away.

"Some—something like that."

"Mama's gettin' married, mama's gettin' married," Aria sang, skipping around.

When she saw the albino, she wondered why her mother would marry such a man. Even though his clothes to her were very nice, his presence felt so cold and clammy, it made Aria's skin itch.

"Stop that!" Miranda scolded, moving her scratching hand. "And say hello to the nice man. This is him. The one I told you about."

Cautiously, Aria stepped forward and held out her hand, but instead of shaking it, he kissed it then spoke to her in French.

"You talk funny." Aria snickered.

He smiled.

"That is French. I will teach you to speak it soon. I said, you are very pretty," he explained, even though he had really said, you taste so sweet. Miranda spoke Creole, a derivation of French; she knew what he said but tricked herself into believing she didn't. She needed to believe the lie she told herself about what this forty-year-old man wanted with her eight-year-old daughter.

"Thank you." Aria blushed, swallowing the compliment and twirling.

He looked at her mother. "She is all that you said she would be."

Miranda fought back tears of guilt. "Please take good care of her," she whispered.

Satan ran his thumb over her lips, causing a quiver.

"Didn't I take good care of you?"

She sucked his thumb into her mouth and nodded. He held out his hand to Aria.

"Come, my child. I have a surprise for you."

Aria, trusting her mother, allowed him to pick her up and carry her off. She would never see her mother again...

#########

By the second day on the roof, Aria felt deathly ill. Her whole body was weak, and she had a delirious fever. It had come from sitting in those wet clothes, viruses jumping out of the water, becoming toxic and airborne. She felt like she was going to die.

She heard a distant buzz . . . like a dragonfly's wings getting closer and closer, until she realized it was a boat. She squinted, and in the distance saw the small motorboat powering toward her.

"Thank you, God," she whispered weakly.

But she couldn't be thankful long.

It was a sheriff's boat. On it was one middle-aged redneck sheriff. His mirrored sunglasses and toothpick made him look like he was straight out of central casting.

He cut off the boat and coasted over to her, then tossed a rope around the chimney to anchor him to the spot.

"Well, lil' lady, seems like I'm right on time." He chuckled. "You sick?"

She nodded weakly.

"Y-y-yes."

"Guess you're lucky I came this way. We thought we'd cleared everybody from this area. Yesss . . . lucky indeed."

Aria looked up at the sheriff. She had been with enough men to damn near take their temperature with a glance. It was clear this one had jungle fever.

"You sho' are pretty. What is ya? Creole gal?"

She knew what he wanted, but she also knew what she could give him . . . a bullet between the eyes. She knew his body wouldn't be found until after the storm, but she knew she couldn't just take a Sheriff's boat. It would be like making a police cruiser your getaway car. Besides, if she said no, he'd probably take it anyway, and then he'd probably harass her, take her bag. Then she'd have to kill him.

"I'm whatever you want me to be," she said without flirtation, but inviting enough to make him smile.

He fumbled with his zipper, looking around.

"I ain't asking much, just a little kiss for ol' Billy Bob here." He chuckled.

He pulled out his pale sausage-like dick. Aria scooted over along the edge of the roof until she was between his legs.

"A tongue kiss, if you don't mind," he leered.

She took his limpness in her mouth. Even sick, her head game had him brick hard by mid bob. She used her tongue to tickle and tease his head.

"Ohhh yeah, ain't nothin' wetter than the mouth of a nigger bitch," the sheriff grunted.

Aria had to fight the urge to bite this cracker's dick off.

"Watch the teeth," he hissed, glaring down at her, grabbing a handful of her hair.

The heat of her angry humiliation and her being completely numb carried her through the act. When he came, she started to spit it out, but he held her in place firmly and growled, "Now swallow."

It was the hardest gulp of her life, but after that, she would be able to swallow anything.

The sheriff smiled and patted her on the head like she was a poodle.

"Good gal. Sho' wish, we'd met under better conditions . . . Coulda got better acquainted." He smirked.

"Me too," she replied, her fever like a candle in the sun compared to her inner rage.

He jerked his head. "Come on. Get in."

He watched her grab her book bag and get in. He unleashed the chimney.

"What you got in the bag, gal?"

"Johnny the Conqueror, Brick Dust . . . Bones," she replied.

He laughed as he started the motor.

"I knew you were Creole! Got me ah ol' conjurer woman, ha? Gonna cast a spell on ol' skeeter, ha? Hell, you already cast one on ol' Billy Bob!"

Aria glanced at the back of his head with murderous intent. Hold that thought, she told herself.

############

The Superdome.

. . . But she had never seen it like this. It looked like something out of an end of the world type movie. People were living in the parking lot, lying around as if their worlds had exploded, and the blast had blown them there like rubble and debris.

It had.

Inside it was even worse. The stench alone smelled of death, sickness, fear and despair. Moving through the motley mass made Aria feel like she finally understood the concept of hell. She turned the book bag around in front of her, so she could keep an eye on it. She knew if anyone even thought she had money in the bag, they'd tear her to pieces getting at it. The place was filled with good people, families, the spirit of love and brotherhood could be seen in the warm smiles and welcoming hugs for strangers.

But that was only half of it.

The other half was the dark and diabolical, the leers, the sneers, the murderers, rapists, and thieves. The county jail had flooded and most, if not all the inmates not moved to Angola, escaped. Many sought refuge in the cracks and crevices of the Superdome, because it was impossible for the authorities to police, so the Superdome had a law all its own.

The law of the jungle.

Aria felt the hand over her mouth and the arm around her throat. She wanted to fight, but all she felt were hands on her feet, arms, and legs.

They had been watching her since she arrived a few hours earlier.

"Fresh meat," the leader cackled.

There were five of them. All were escapees. Three rapists, one murderer, and the leader, a hybrid, a rapist and a murderer. They preyed on the weak women and men. Once they saw she was unprotected, they pounced.

People saw them, as they had many times before. But no one wanted to get involved, so they turned a blind eye. Once Aria felt herself firmly restrained, she let her body go limp.

"This bitch ain't even fightin', whoadie!" one of the rapists exclaimed, dick hardening.

"All bitches want it," another added.

They all knew they were the predator and she, the prey.

They carried her into their bathroom. Inside were two other dudes smoking a blunt. When they saw the pretty young thing the crew had caught, the blunt was forgotten.

"I'm next!"

"Fuck that nigguh, I'm next!"

"Man, fuck all y'all! This my bitch! I might not let none of y'all get none," the leader barked, flexing his large prison muscles.

"Come on, Slim, don't be like that!"

Seeing her lie there on the floor of the darkened bathroom quietly, made them forget all about holding her. No one heard the slow zzzzzzzzzzzz of the book bag, just enough to get her hand in. She pulled out one of the .45's and kicked the safety off, then held it concealed under her thigh.

Her smile said she was toying with them.

"Come on, Slim, what you waitin' for?" she cooed, making her N'awlin's accent extra thick, "Don't you want some of this, huh?"

Slim licked his lips, taking out his dick. "Hell yeah."

Her smile disappeared, like somebody snatching a needle off a record.

"Then I'ma damn sure give it to you."

When Slim saw the gleam of that thing in her hand, his smile disappeared too, and "Oh shitttt," slipped from his lips.

And shit he did, because when the first shot blew his dick off and the other blew through his eye and out the top of his brain, his bowels emptied themselves as soon as he fell dead to the floor.

"Oh shit! The bitch got—"

Boc! Boc! Boc! Boc!

Four shots, four nigguhs' ass, four screams of agony like a quartet of pain. Aria quickly snatched out the other .45. The other two dudes cowered in the corner.

"Who's next?" she asked calmly. "Didn't you say you were next?"

"No, no, ple—"

Boc!

Head cracked. Brains on the ceiling. Body on the floor. Aria laughed.

"Oh now, nobody want next, huh? Fuck it, you next!"

Boc!

"And you!"

Boc!

"And you and you and you!"

Boc! Boc! Boc!

The whole bathroom smelled like blood, shit, and gun smoke. She let the empty clips fall to the floor, then pulled out fresh ones and reloaded. Only two of the seven were still alive, one was shot in the leg, the other in the arm. She squatted down next to them.

"I – I – I ain't have nothin' to do—" he stammered.

"I – I – I don't want to hear it," Aria spat, mocking his stammer. "I have one question. You want to live?"

He nodded so hard, she thought he'd get whiplash.

"Okay . . . suck his dick."

His eyes got big. She grabbed him by the throat and put the gun to his forehead.

"Okay, okay, okay, I'll do it!" he shouted.

"Do it."

As soon as he pulled his man's dick out and put it in his mouth, she raised the gun.

Boc! Boc!

And he died with a dick in his mouth.

"Fuckin' animal, you don't deserve to live," she murmured as she headed out the bathroom.

Within several hours, word had spread all over the Superdome about what she had done. It let the other predators know the little cinnamon honey with her hand in the book bag—she ain't to be fucked with . . .

Not only the predators, but the prey had a reaction.

"I—I've got some water. You want some?" a lanky but curvy chocolate female asked Aria.

She was tired of being harassed, so she clung to Aria like a security blanket. Two more females approached. By the end of the day, five females were rotating around her as if she were the sun. But it wasn't for free. She made them work the only thing they had. Their bodies. Within three days, Aria had a tent, a supply of water, and hydrated food, all courtesy of her stable. She learned right then how it felt to be man and woman and it was a lesson she'd put to good use.

On the fifth day, she saw her.

The high yellow girl with the chubby face and the blood red hair. She had noticed her because of the red hair and the fact that all she seemed to do was sleep. Until the fly landed on her face. That's when she knew she was dead. She kept a purse clutched to her chest. Aria went over to her. Shoved her shoulder. When she felt the stiffness, it only confirmed what she already knew.

Aria snatched the purse from her dead clutch and rummaged through it. No money, no credit card, but she found her birth certificate and social security card.

It read Jazmine Coleman.

A smile spread on her face.

"Jazmine . . . I like it!"

##########

Ten days in, she started to worry. Every day she prayed, prayed that Swag would come, but with every passing day, she felt more and more that Satan had got him.

"What's wrong, Jaz?" her chocolate ho asked.

"Nothin'," she grumbled.

But the pain was getting harder to hide.

Until . . .

Lying in her tent, her face tasting astro turf, finger 'pon cock, she heard the swamp cry. At first, she thought she was dreaming because she had dreamed of the sound before. So, she rolled over and kept—She heard it again . . . louder.

Her eyes popped open. She put the bag on, facing front, and stepped out. The usual buzz of noises echoed. But over it all she heard the call of the swamp. Aria couldn't do it, even though Swag had tried to teach her, but she could sing. So sing she did.

She let loose a note that bubbled low and then fluttered high, making the drone of voices stop on a dime, because her voice sounded like the sun rising.

When she heard the swamp cry the third time, she knew it was him . . . and then she saw him. She took off, stepping over bodies, knocking over set ups, leaning tents until she beat a path straight to him and jumped dead in his arms, damn near knocking him over.

He laughed as she covered his face with kisses.

"If this is how you act when I leave, I must go more often."

"And I'll kill you!" She laughed. "What took you so long?"

"Just a little storm." He smirked. "But not even a hurricane could keep me from you."

"I love you," she breathed, then kissed him.

"Come, we must get out of New Orleans. We can leave the city now. I have transportation."

"Okay, but first, I have a man I need to see at the sheriff's office," she replied with death in her eyes.

She had held the thought . . .

<h1 style="text-align:center">-29-</h1>

Milly, Lilly, and Miss Toni all hung from chains, extended from the ceiling and wrapped around their wrists. Their feet were only touching the floor because they were on their tippy toes. It made their calves and toes ache like they were running a marathon. But when they took the weight off and just dangled by their arms, it felt as if their shoulders were being pulled out of their sockets. It was excruciating, just as Satan had intended it to be.

Two of his goons stood aside while Satan stood center stage. He glanced at his watch, then after listening to their groans a few more minutes, he said, "Why are you doing this to yourselves? We're on the same side; we want the same thing. You want Swag and so do I. You tell me where he is, help me set him up, and I'll take care of it. I have no problem with you, so *why* are you making problems for me?"

"Pussy bwoy!" Milly barked, then spat at Satan.

It landed a few feet from the tip of his gators.

"You're lucky you have bad aim," he remarked.

"You–you–you might as well do—do what you gonna d—do," Miss Toni gritted, "because we ain't telling you shit!"

Satan shrugged with amused resignation.

"I guess the old saying isn't absolute. The enemy of my enemy isn't always my friend," he remarked, then turned to his goons. "Do it."

One goon walked off into the shadows of the room, then came back with a chainsaw. Milly, Lilly, and Miss Toni couldn't hide the look of fear emanating from their guts, until it molded their expression.

"Exactly . . . I don't want to take it there either," Satan said smoothly. "So please . . . can we all just . . . get along?"

"I-I don't say this often, b-but you can sssssuck my dick," Miss Toni spat.

Satan laughed. "I'm sure you don't, sweetie."

When the chainsaw roared to life, it sounded like a hideous beast, irritated by being awakened from its sleep. The spinning blade, swapping and biting, hungry for a taste of flesh.

"One more chance . . . feed the beast."

The goon approached Milly first. He held the chain up to her waist. She turned to Lilly, one last time and shouted, "I love—"

"Youuuuuuuu!" Lilly completed as the chainsaw tore into Milly's rib cage. Some twins are so close they feel each other's pain, *literally*. Milly and Lilly were those kinds of twins. When the chainsaw began to slice through Milly's mid-section, she didn't cry out. Lilly did.

"Aaaaarrrggghhh nooooo!" she bellowed excruciatingly.

It was as if the chainsaw was ripping apart her intestines, severing her spine and ripping open her gut. Milly simply dangled, eyes rolled up in the back of her head as if she were in a voodoo trance, shaking and trembling. Black bile and blood bubbled from her mouth, frothing and dripping as her lower half was completely separated and dropped to the floor like a side of beef.

The experience gave Lilly a heart attack, stopping her heart instantly. Her head dropped and she was gone. Milly still clung to life, even though she was now only half the woman she used to be.

"Life never ceases to amaze me," Satan said with genuine admiration, then lifted his gun and put a hole in Milly's head, ending her useless string of babble.

When Miss Toni saw Milly's body looking like something out of a horror flick right before his eyes—intestines falling out of her with wet slurpy slaps on the floor, he threw up until he only retched but nothing came out. He had never seen anything like it, and it fucked his head up.

You're next, his mind panicked. *Just tell this nigguh what he wants to know!* But his heart wouldn't let him violate the principles he lived by, especially now that the twins had died for them, too. To do so now, would make their death in vain, and he was too much of a loyal bitch to do that.

Satan stepped over to him.

"Baby listen . . . we can end it here. I need someone like you on my team. Let's not waste a beautiful opportunity." Satan smiled.

Toni, all the Miss part gone, mustering every ounce of manhood he had left, looked at Satan, smiled and replied, "How you still talking with my dick in your mouth?" Then he laughed hysterically, psyching himself up.

Satan's jaw flexed with irritation. He snatched the chainsaw from his goon, revved it hard, then put it within a millimeter of Toni's face.

"I'm going to enjoy this," he seethed.

Toni only laughed harder . . . until Satan sliced off his foot at the ankle.

"Ahhhhhhhhhhhh ha!" Toni screamed, but the scream soon turned back into a maniacal laugh.

Satan sliced off his other foot. Toni started singing, "Footloose! Footloose! Everybody cut footloose!"

He had psyched his mind into a place beyond the pain. He knew it would be all over soon. He comforted himself by thinking of his mother's smile and how he'd be with her in heaven soon. Or . . . if he were headed to hell, how he'd be with his sorry ass uncle, the man who molested all of his manhood out of him before he knew what it meant to even be a man, and then he'd give him a taste of his own medicine for all of eternity.

"Talk, nigguh!" Satan barked.

"I'm talking to youuuuu, come on!" Toni sang loudly, tears of pain burning his cheeks.

Satan cut off one of his arms. Toni dangled by one arm, his shoulder snapping and dislocating.

"That's all you got, huh? Come on!" Toni barked.

Satan lowered the chainsaw.

". . . yes . . . I could've really used you on the team," he remarked, admiringly. Then with one swoop, he cut Toni's head off and watched it drop and fall at his feet.

"Stay on the precinct. She'll come back to work soon, and then she'll lead us right to him, I guarantee!" Satan was right back to square one in finding Jasmine.

-31-

Dolla pulled his Land Rover up to the curb, right in front of the prostitute with the long blonde wig, soft cinnamon complexion, and sexy body.

She leaned in the passenger window. "Lookin' for some action, daddy?" She winked.

He chuckled. "You tell me."

She tossed away the cigarette in her hand, then got in. He pulled away, glancing at her with amusement.

"I like your style, Detective."

Jazmine smiled. "We can't have the streets saying you're working with the police, can we? That's why I had you meet me on the stroll, because believe me, things are about to get deep."

Dolla's expression changed from amused to worried.

"Look, I ain't tryin' to get *deep*. I told you what I knew about the dude. That's it."

"No, Dolla, it's not it. This guy Swag is a menace. Now we both have an interest in seeing him out of commission, right?" Jazmine reasoned.

"Yeah but—"

"No buts, you scratch my back and I scratch yours," she replied, then used her nails to scratch his neck and send a shiver down his spine, then cooed, "How's that feel?"

He glanced over at her, taking in her micro mini and thick juicy thighs. *Damn she sexy*, he thought.

Jazmine felt the same way. He had a smooth cinnamon complexion with brown eyes, and they were about the same height.

"I'm just sayin', Detect—"

"Call me Jaz."

"I'm just sayin', Jaz, I ain't tryin' to get deep," he repeated.

"Don't worry, I've got your back. But understand this, I'm a by the book cop. If you get out of line, I will bust that ass," she stated firmly.

Sometimes, the best way to be dirty is to pretend you're clean . . .

"I'm just a hustler, ma, tryin' to make a dollar out of fifteen cents," he replied humbly.

She laughed. "Believe me, I know what you do. Just don't let me see you do it."

"I got you."

"Make a right and let me out," Jazmine instructed.

When he did, she opened the door and gave him her most sexy look. "Maybe, when this is over, you and I can ummmm . . . have a drink?"

Then innuendo started the fantasy rolling in his head. "Shit, we can do that now."

She laughed sweetly, incitingly, then got out taking his desires tied to her little finger.

##########

"I'm glad you could come," Sonia said with a warm smile as she opened the door.

"I came as soon as I could," Jazmine replied, stepping inside.

Jazmine could tell Sonia needed to talk when she called her asking about the progress of the case. The way she dragged the conversation out, Jazmine knew Sonia had something on her mind. Jazmine did, too. Rain had schooled her on the situation between Matson and Sonia, so she was eager to pick Sonia's brain and see how she could use the situation to her advantage.

"Can I get you something? Coffee? Something stronger?"

"Coffee's fine," Jazmine replied.

They sat at the kitchen table, cups of coffee steaming in front of them.

"I . . . I'm sure Tony explained the . . . situation to you," Sonia began.

"Vaguely," Jazmine lied, seeing what Sonia would use as a defense. Sonia looked into her cup, then back at Jazmine.

"The money . . . came from Love. This is true. We had an affair."

"I see. But, why did he send you money in such a roundabout way? Excuse me for asking, affairs are all about discretion. Not paper trails."

Sonia took a deep breath.

". . . it's for child support. He's Bianca's father."

"Wow!" Jazmine remarked, acting as if she didn't know. "How did Tony take it?"

Sonia wiped away a tear. "He . . . he wants a divorce."

"What about you?"

Without hesitation, Sonia said, "I want my marriage."

Jazmine reached across the table, took her hand, and gave it a squeeze.

"Give him time. Space. He loves you, but I'm sure you can understand something like this takes time to swallow."

Sonia nodded, sipped her coffee and leaned back in her seat. "Will, you tell me something . . . and be totally honest."

"Of course," Jazmine lied.

Sonia looked her in the eyes.

"Do you think I'll ever see my daughter again?"

The question totally threw Jazmine. She didn't expect it, nor did she expect the prayerful, yet stoic look in Sonia's eyes. It was the look of a mother who loved her daughter deeply, who yearned for her return, but for her own sanity, had to prepare for the worst.

She would have never given Bianca away, Jazmine's heart whispered, and at first she felt resentful because her mother *had* given her away. Then, she softened and replied, "I . . . I don't know, Sonia. But I do know the department is doing all it can."

Sonia nodded, and forcing a weak smile. She then wiped at her tears.

"Can I see her room?" Jazmine asked, surprising herself with the request.

"Sure."

She didn't know why she had asked until she saw the room. It was done up in pink and purple, the typical little girl's room, unicorns and rainbows, the budding expression of feminine energy, bold but unsure, timid but curious, open but hidden in her own self-spinning mystery. The space where little girls can be themselves.

Jazmine knew, even if Bianca did make it back, this room wouldn't fit her anymore. The world had shown her what was truly behind the mask, and she knew Bianca would never be the same.

In Bianca's mirror, Jazmine looked at herself and saw herself as Bianca saw herself. And then she could see Bianca *in* her reflection. See what Bianca could become if someone didn't save her, and it made her shudder. *Nobody saved us*, her mind huffed.

But we wished they had, her heart replied.

Seeing Bianca in her reflection made Jazmine break down in tears.

"Jazmine! Are you okay?" Sonia questioned, rushing to her side.

Jazmine couldn't even respond. The tears were so strong, strong because they had been a long time coming. She had never truly cried for herself; she had been too busy surviving. But now she had, and she knew what she had to do.

Jazmine finally regained her composure, looked at Sonia and *vowed*, "I will get your daughter back."

The determination in her tone sent a chill of joy down Sonia's spine.

"I believe you!"

The two women embraced. Sonia cried tears of joy and pain. Joy, because she felt Jazmine's words all over. But pain because, smelling her perfume, she now knew exactly who *she* was . . .

-32-

"Yo, I'm hungry as shit, whoadie."

"Shit, me too. You got another blunt?"

"Yeah . . . hold up."

The two goons sat in the car across the street from the police precinct. They were under strict orders to bring Jazmine to Satan the minute she showed up at work. She hadn't been there in over a week, but they weren't about to move until the next set of goons came and relieved their shift.

"What time is it?" the passenger asked, lighting the blunt.

"We got 'bout another hour," the driver answered, casually glancing in the rearview.

He saw a bag lady pushing a cart up the street, talking to herself and staggering wildly.

"Look whoadie." The driver chuckled. "That's how your mama gonna be, she keep fuckin' wit' that wet."

"Nigguh, fuck you!" The passenger laughed and passed him the blunt. The bag lady pushed her cart alongside the driver's side. The goon glanced up as she staggered and ran the cart into his bumper.

The goon rolled down his window.

"Aight, bitch. Watch where—" That was all he got out. The bag lady pulled out a .45 automatic and put it to his forehead.

"Don't fuckin' *move!*" Swag hissed.

At the same time a van skidded up and two gunmen jumped out, aiming their guns at the passenger. The whole thing happened so fast, neither goon had time to react. One second, they were smoking a blunt, the next they were face down in the van surrounded by nigguhs with attitudes and guns . . .

Swag snatched off the rags she had on and put her gun to the driver's head.

"Ay yo, watch this," Swag told the passenger.

Boc!

The bullets exploding in his brain sounded as squishy as a boot stepping in the mud. Blood shot out and hit the passenger in the eye.

"Fuck!" the passenger barked, hands pinned behind his back, so he couldn't even wipe his face.

Swag put the gun to his head. "Now you know I'm not playin'," she spat. "I'm only askin' you once. Where's Satan?"

"I-I-I'll take you to him!" he blurted out.

##########

Matson rolled over and stared at the motel ceiling. In his mind's eye, he saw Rain and Sonia's face, side by side, each looking back at him with the same questioning expression.

There was no denying his love for Sonia. They had too much history. Just because a person made a mistake, even a *big* mistake, you didn't just stop loving them, you didn't stop *wanting* to love them either.

But a man's pride can be an obstacle in any decision, and he knew it was coloring his thought process.

Then there was Rain. He knew she was really feeling him, and the feeling was mutual, but there was so much more involved. Namely, Jazmine. Matson knew Rain and Jazmine were in a relationship, but what else were they involved in? There was no doubt in his mind about Jazmine's dirt, but was Rain just along for the ride, or was she involved, too?

His phone began to beep wildly. It was the GPS program. It meant one of the chips was on the move. He snatched the phone up and saw the blip moving through the city.

"It's the motorcycle," he mumbled, jumping up to put his shoes on.

Since he had tagged the bike, it hadn't moved. He was beginning to think maybe somebody had found the chip. But now, seeing it move across the screen, he knew he had hit pay dirt.

"Tonight I find out who the fuck is under the helmet," he remarked as he grabbed his keys and headed out the door.

##########

Swag pulled up at the warehouse and parked the motorcycle in the shadows. She looked up at the three-story brick warehouse, its entire backside sitting right on the river. She knew it was exactly the type of place Satan would use for his operation.

She walked back a block to where the van was parked. Swag jumped in the back, where several of her Pink Diamond thugs were masked up, locked and loaded. The goon lay on the floor tied up.

"He wasn't lyin'. This is definitely the place," Swag reported.

"You gonna let me go now?" the goon asked eagerly.

"Yeah," Swag replied, then put the silenced .45 to his dome and blew his brains out. "Bye."

His body jerked and twitched, but no one paid attention. All they wanted to know was, "You think he got the coke here?"

They wanted their stolen coke back.

"Definitely," Swag lied, not knowing and not caring about the coke. She had come for Bianca. "Remember, use the silencers until you absolutely have to use the big guns. This nigguh got a team like roaches. Once they on us, they swarm."

They all nodded, took breaths, and psyched themselves up.

"Let's do this!"

Swag smiled and led the way.

#########

Matson followed the blip to the warehouse. He drove by, squinting into the darkness but saw nothing. He circled the block once they parked and walked back. He found the bike but no rider.

"What the hell is here?" he mumbled, then he heard a gunshot and all hell broke loose.

#########

Swag and her eight-man team dressed in all black and moving like Ninjas, managed to take out the first three guards on the outside with silenced shots.

All that was heard was clumping bodies.

Swag grabbed the doorman and put the gun to his head.

"Open the door!" Swag gritted.

"Fuck you!"

Ssssspppt!

His brains quietly leaked like a rusty faucet. She opened the door herself. Peeped in. Waved her team in. They entered and fanned out, infrareds crisscrossing the darkened room like a laser show.

"Hey!" a goon yelled when he came around the corner and spotted them.

Sssssppppt!

The single shot silenced him like a mummy. They stepped over him and came to a staircase leading up and down. Swag put her finger to her mouth and listened. She heard the drone of voices coming from below. She pointed down. The team descended, foot over foot, backs flat against the wall.

When they came to the bottom of the stairs, Swag peeked around the corner and a slight smile spread across her face. She saw the rows and rows of cages filled with naked females. She saw one guard.

"Psssst!" she called and got his attention.

When he looked, all he saw was a red light and a rhino bullet flying at him.

Splat!

His brains came out of his ear and painted the wall.

Swag and her team entered the room.

"Blow the locks off these cages," Swag ordered.

"Yo Swag, we here for coke, not pussy!" one Pink Diamond thug objected.

Before Swag could respond, an automatic weapon ripped through the air, sounding like a typewriter, 100 words a minute.

Bbbbrrrrrrpppppppp!

That was the gunshot Matson heard.

He snatched out his weapon and then his cellphone. He had no signal because of the steel and concrete all around.

"Shit!"

He needed to call for backup because that first gunshot had proven to be the first note of a murderous melody. His car was parked a block away, so he couldn't get to his radio, and his cop instinct was telling him he couldn't wait. He had to go in alone.

When Matson got to the back entrance, he saw the four dead men scattered like leaves around the door.

Bbbrrrrrttttt! Bbbbbrrrrrrr!

The automatic weapons roared like they were having an argument. Matson stepped inside. Another body. A figure dressed in all black came up the stairs.

"Freeze!" Matson barked.

The figure raised his weapon. Matson fired.

Boc!

The figure tumbled back down the stairs. Matson came behind it. All the gun fire was coming from down there. When he peeped around the corner and saw all the females in the cages, his heart leaped out of his chest and exploded from his throat, with a resounding, "Bianca! Bianca Matson, it's daddy!"

He came out blazing like a mad man, mowing down Pink Diamond Thugs and goons alike. He stayed low, going cage to cage.

"Bianca, Bianca baby, please be here!"

Boc! Boc! Boc!

He gunned down two more goons. They were everywhere. He picked up a fallen AK-47 and went Rambo on four more.

Bbbbrrrrrhhhhhh!

They fell like bouncing pins. He spotted another staircase and heard gunfire above. He took the stairs two at a time.

#########

Swag moved swiftly. She was in a zone. Almost like in a video game, she was picking off goons left and right, reloading, snatching extra weapons from dead hands. On the second floor, her footsteps were padded by carpet. She heard the muffled thumps of a gang of footsteps. She ducked into the room, then watched them run past.

When they were gone, she re-emerged, stopped, sniffed. She knew he was near. She smelled the incense. Carefully, she cased each room until she came to the end of the hall. She listened at the door and heard the sounds of girlish giggles.

Swag kicked in the door.

Bianca and Alicia were naked in bed, lying in a warm embrace, motherly but erotic. Bianca's breath caught in her throat when she saw the armed man, but Alicia's didn't. In fact, in one glance, she knew it wasn't a man at all. Despite the green contacts, she saw right through to her hazel gaze. She knew her aura too well, knew her presence. Her body had been blossomed and turned out by her, so she'd recognize her even if she had gone blind.

Swag knew her instantly, as well. In the short time, the instant they looked at each other, a whole conversation transpired.

Aria . . .

Alicia . . .

Why?

Don't make me do this.

I love you, but I belong to him.

Noooooooo!

Alicia reached for the gun on the table. Swag didn't hesitate, but her heart felt like it had been ripped from her chest as she fired.

Boc! Boc!

Both shots hit Alicia center mass, dead in the heart like it was a bull's-eye. The gun fell from her dead hand, her eyes glazed like a doll, and she slumped against the headboard.

A tear ran down Swag's cheek. She hated that she had just killed her. All she could see was the little girl she once was, the little girl she had turned into a monster.

In reality, she had killed her long ago . . .

Bianca screamed. "Nooooo! Why did you kill her? Why?"

Swag hugged her tightly. "Shhhh, don't cry, baby. It's over, it's all over," Swag said, but the voice wasn't a man's.

"You're right . . . it is."

Swag heard the voice, but before she could react, she felt the cold steel to her head.

"Stand . . . up."

Swag released Bianca and rose slowly. Bianca ran and slipped under the bed. Swag raised her hands.

"A'ight, you got a winner," Swag said, voice firmly in place.

Satan chuckled. "Turn around and drop your weapon."

She did.

"So . . . *Swag*, I presume."

"Who you 'posed to be?" Swag grilled him.

Satan laughed. "I'm sure you already know," he replied, then tucked his gun, stepping toward Swag, saying, "I'm going to enjoy this."

Swag swung at Satan, but he whacked her arm away like he was swatting a fly and backhanded blood from her mouth. She spun like a top and slammed into the wall. Before she could hit the floor, he grabbed her by the throat, pinning her to the spot.

"You think you can fool me with a dime store disguise?" He cackled, snatching her moustache and goatee off so hard, she cried out.

Jazmine?

The word exploded in Matson's mind when Satan unmasked her. He couldn't believe his eyes.

As soon as he had hit the stairs, he was able to get a signal. He quickly called for backup.

"Detective Matson. And I need back up ASAP. Send SWAT. I repeat, send SWAT! I'm in the warehouse district, pier nine!"

Coming up the stairs, he ran into the five goons that Swag had ducked. His AK-47 was a broom and they were dirt that got swept away with one laughing cackle from the AK-47.

Then he heard the scream.

There was no doubt that, that was Bianca's scream. He moved into the hallway and saw the big albino enter the room at the end of the hall. Quickly, he moved down the hall, positioning himself right outside the door. He didn't see Bianca, but he did hear Satan say, "So *Swag*, I presume."

Swag? he thought. *But wasn't Swag dead?*

But when Satan snatched off her disguise, he had to keep from blurting out, "Jazmine?"

Seeing Satan choking her, he found himself hoping, *praying*, that he would kill her. Kill her on the spot. It would solve all his problems. No more blackmail, he could have Rain all to himself, and no one would ever know his wife was fucking the city's number one drug boss.

Kill her! Kill the bitch! His mind urged, until he heard . . .

"I—I came for the girl!"

"What girl?" Satan seethed, easing his grip enough for her to speak.

"Bianca," she answered.

His frown hardened into a smile. "You mean, *my* daughter."

"No. *I'm* your daughter. Take me . . . take me in her place and let her go," she offered.

Satan looked in her eyes, saw she was serious. He let her go and laughed.

"You're serious, aren't you? What makes you so sure I want you?"

She smirked and stood up.

"Because you came all this way to get me."

His smile disappeared.

"I came all this way for *revenge*! Did you think you could run from me? Did he think he could take you? You were *both* fools. I knew what he would do before *he* did! That's why he spared Love in New Orleans. He thought he could use Love to his advantage, but I used him to mine!" Satan chuckled, "It's ironic . . . I offered Love the exact thing I was going to have him killed for. A part of the heroin trade in New Orleans."

She frowned.

She hadn't known Swag had made a deal with Love.

"So, you had your own son killed?"

"Oh, he told you. I figured he would, but I also figured he wouldn't tell you everything," he replied.

"Everything?" she echoed.

Satan smiled. "So, you'd be willing to trade your life for hers?"

"Yes."

"And why should I agree, when I already have you both?"

She walked up on him and replied, "Because I will never submit if you don't, and that's what you want. That's what you've always wanted. But you could never break me like the rest, could you . . . Daddy?" she cooed, caressing his dick through his pants.

Outside the door, Matson was sick. After all the games, all the manipulation, despite that fact that he had come to despise her, she was willing to lay down her life for his daughter. That, he couldn't ignore. He couldn't turn away. He could no longer hate her.

In the background, the sirens wailed loudly. Satan's ears perked up.

"You bitch!" he spat, then hit her so hard he knocked her out.

He turned for the door. Matson popped up.

"Freeze!"

Satan laughed.

Boc! Boc!

. . . But not for long.

Both shots hit him high in the chest, sending him stumbling backward. He turned his torso, using his momentum and dove headfirst out of the window.

Bianca screamed.

Matson ran over to the window and looked out. Below was the river, the moonlight reflected in it. He tried to remember if he'd heard a splash but hearing Bianca's scream blacked out everything.

"Bianca!"

"Daddy!"

"Bianca!"

"Daddy!" she yelled, scrambling from under the bed and into his waiting arms.

As soon as he wrapped his arms around her, he broke down in sobs. He knew right then it didn't matter who her father was, he was her daddy. He loved her unconditionally and nothing would ever change that.

"I love you, Daddy!"

"I love you, baby!"

Matson finally noticed that she was naked, and it broke his heart. He snatched the blanket off the bed and wrapped it around her, then looked her in the eyes.

"Listen, baby, I know you've been through a lot, but everything is going to be okay, all right?"

She nodded, crying.

Matson looked at Jazmine. He heard the voices and walkie-talkies of approaching officers. Something made him snatch up her moustache and goatee and put it back on her face.

Bianca watched without saying a word.

"Police, freeze!"

"It's me Matson, Detective Matson!" he barked, waving his badge.

"Is everything under control here, Detective?" the SWAT captain asked.

"Yeah, but I want the river dragged ASAP. We're looking for an albino male's body."

"Yes sir. What about him?" the captain asked, pointing at Swag.

"Cuff him, but hold him for me," Matson replied, smirking to himself.

#########

Most of the females that had been kidnapped had been found, including Tosha and the waitress. Unfortunately, several more had already been sold. News cameras were everywhere, a police helicopter scanned the river and a police boat dragged the river.

"Sir, we've been over the whole area with a fine-tooth comb. We didn't find a body," the officer informed Matson.

Matson, still carrying his daughter, sighed with frustration.

"Okay," he gritted, looking out at the river, knowing that Satan was still out there.

"Bianca!"

Matson and Bianca looked and saw Sonia and Felecity running up. He had called her. He didn't want to wait to tell her. The four of them shared a family hug.

"Thank God! Oh, thank *God!*" Sonia cried, wetting her daughter's face with her tears.

"Yeah . . . thank God," he mumbled sincerely. "They still need to take her to the hospital."

Sonia nodded. "O-okay. Are you coming?"

"As soon as I finish up here."

"Does that mean you're coming home?" Sonia asked with anxious eyes.

He caressed her cheek with his thumb. "Yes," he replied, then kissed her forehead.

She exhaled. "I love you."

"I know."

Once Sonia and the kids left, he went and got into his car. He was already told that he had a package waiting on him. Swag was in the back. He looked at Swag through the rearview.

"Swag, right? I've heard a lot about you," Matson remarked, pulling off.

Jazmine was sick. She knew she couldn't go to jail. Once they stripped her, they'd know who she was and then it was all over. She felt something she never felt before . . .

Desperation.

"Look, you can't take me to jail."

Matson laughed. "Can't? I don't see why not."

"Man, listen, I—I got a lot of connects on the street. I can tell you anything you want to know. Just please, man, don't take me to jail," she begged.

"Don't tell me you're scared. Tough guy like you. What, you think you might get fucked?" he teased.

He was enjoying the moment.

"Yeah yo, just . . . no jail . . . I'll tell you whatever you want to know. Plus, you owe me."

"How is that?"

"I saved your daughter."

Matson swallowed, playing hard not to show emotion. "I need more. What else would make this worth my while?"

Matson drove on for a few more moments without saying a word waiting on Swag.

"The mayor's crooked," Swag blurted out.

She hated to lay her ace in the hole, but drastic times...

He glanced in the rearview.

"Can you prove it?"

"Fuck yeah, yo. He–he works for me."

Matson found a quiet block and pulled over. He got out and got in the backseat. "I'm listening."

"He used to work for Love, but when I took over, I inherited his service."

"Why? You got somethin' on him?"

Swag hesitated. She really didn't want to lose such a valuable piece in her chess game. The mayor was like her queen (ironically).

Matson started to get out. "Yeah man, yeah! I got something on him!"

"Like what?"

"Tapes."

"Sex tapes?"

Swag laughed.

"Naw. Money tapes. Laundering, illegal contributions, the whole nine."

Matson thought for a minute, then said, "So . . . you wanna be my snitch?"

Swag's eyes flashed and teeth gritted.

"Yeah . . . I'ma be your . . . snitch."

Matson smiled. "Nah . . . I'd rather you be my . . . bitch."

Swag frowned. She didn't get it, and in that moment, Matson knew why he kept her secret.

Because now he had the upper hand . . .

-The End-

NEW TITLES FROM WAHIDA CLARK PRESENTS

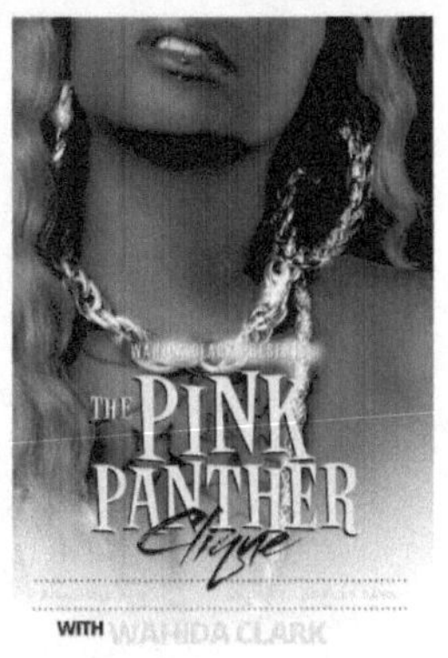

#READIT

WWW.WCLARKPUBLISHING.COM